D1715350

Teeth of the Dog

OTHER BOOKS BY JILL CIMENT

Half a Life

The Law of Falling Bodies

Small Claims

Teeth of the Dog

A NOVEL BY

JILL CIMENT

CROWN PUBLISHERS, INC.
NEW YORK

Grateful acknowledgment is made for permission to reprint from the following:

"Suzanne" by Leonard Cohen. Copyright © 1967 Sony/ATV Songs LLC. (Renewed.) All rights administered by Sony/ATV Music Publishing, 8 Music Square West, Nashville, TN 37203.

"Casabianca" from *The Complete Poems, 1927–1979* by Elizabeth Bishop. Copyright © 1979, 1983 by Alice Helen Methfessel. Reprinted by permission of Farrar, Straus & Giroux, Inc.

Published by Crown Publishers, Inc., 201 East 50th Street, New York, New York 10022. Member of the Crown Publishing Group.

Random House, Inc. New York, Toronto, London, Sydney, Auckland
www.randomhouse.com

Design by Lauren Dong

Printed in the United States of America

Library of Congress Cataloging-in-Publication Data
Ciment, Jill
Teeth of the dog / Jill Ciment. — 1st ed.
I. Title.
PR9199.3.C499T44 1999
813'.54—dc21 98-26453 CIP

ISBN 0-517-70202-9

10 9 8 7 6 5 4 3 2 1

First Edition

For Ann

and, as always, Arnold

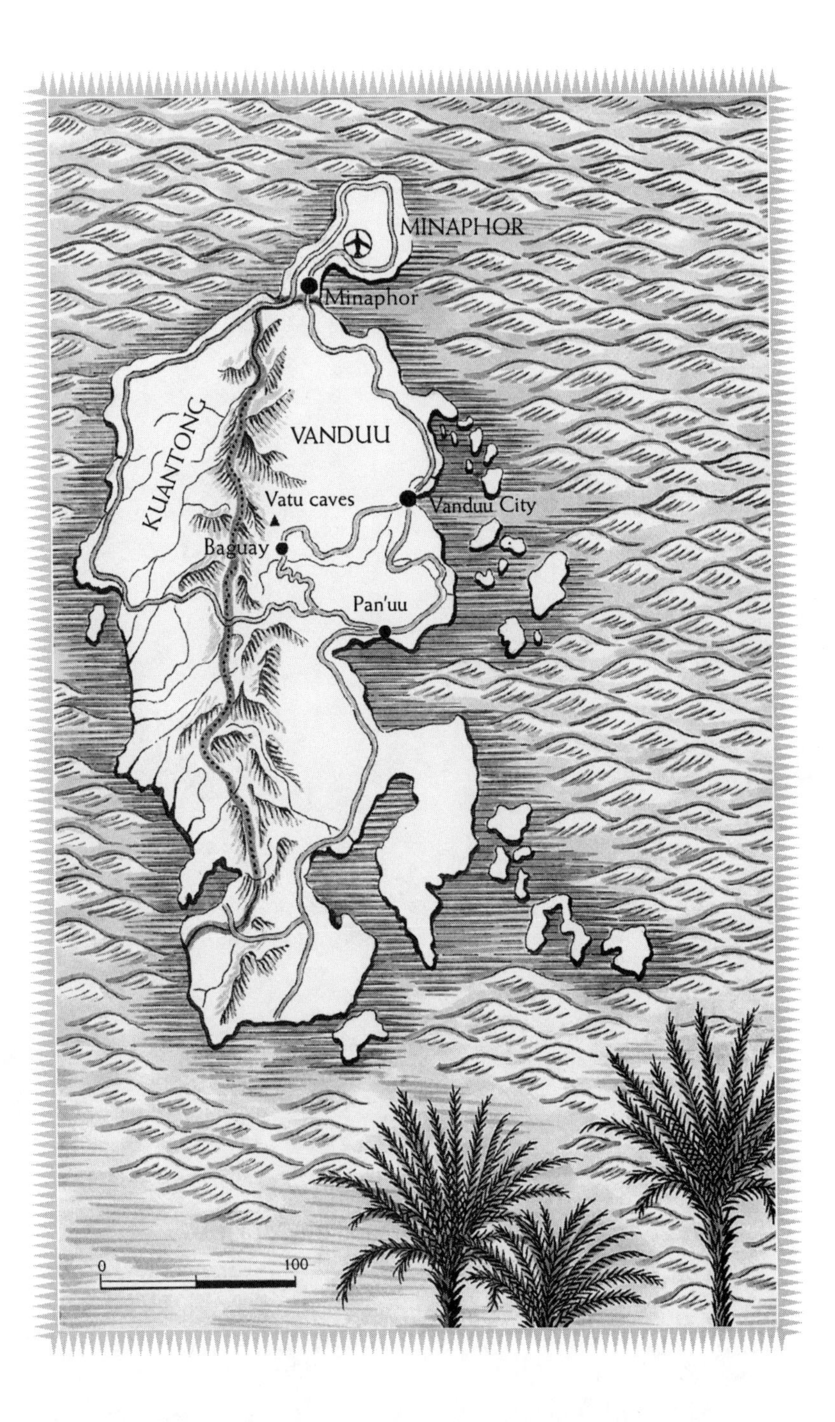
MINAPHOR
Minaphor
KUANTONG
VANDUU
Vatu caves
Vanduu City
Baguay
Pan'uu
0
100

Part One

Finster surveyed the long, volcanic stretch of beach and spotted the rinky-dink ferry boat. It chugged through the surf, spewing out diesel oil. When the sun hit the oil, casting arcs and squiggles of bright iridescent colors on the glassy swells, the drab, peeling ferry appeared to be floating atop another ferry, a bright fun ferry of the netherworld.

Finster snuffed out his Thai stick, slipped on his flip-flops, and trotted across the black sand toward the wharf. Though tourists rarely entered the country by ferry these days, the hawkers had come out anyway—Chinese boys selling Seiko watches with Tinkertoy inner works and a big, sullen family of Indian shopkeepers who had recently fled Fiji. They'd managed to smuggle out the best of their inventory—hand-carved Fijian salad bowls the size of manhole covers.

Finster arrived at the wharf just as the ferry slapped against the pilings and a throng of native passengers started funneling down the gangplank. The old men wore sarongs, but the young ones sported T-shirts that read *Baywatch* or *It's Not Beer, Mate, This Is Just a Fat Shirt.* The Muslim women glided out next, swaddled in flapping lengths of Hawaiian shirt material, followed by a trio of loud, hefty Palauans, a Chinese businessman, and a white couple. Squinting into the eye-frying sun, Finster scrutinized the couple. The old man was very gray and very tall and very concave. The young woman wore a tank top and no bra and her red hair, tossed and stiffened by twelve hours on the sloshing deck, had hardened into a seascape, like one of those Japanese serigraphs where the waves, all foam and power, are forever on the verge of crashing. In a slinky dress, she'd be a knockout, Finster thought. Or maybe he'd lost his connoisseur's eye after six years on this rock and any Occidental woman whose skin didn't turn firecracker red under the relentless sun looked smashing to him.

Mopping the perspiration from his sparse blond mustache, Finster headed up the gangplank toward the ferry's cargo hold, then stopped for a moment to watch the couple—more precisely the woman's breasts—enter the gauntlet of enterprise set up entirely for their perusal. The boys yelled, "Best price, real deal," and dangled their watches in front of the couple's eyes. The Indians sat cross-legged and mute behind their colossal salad bowls. The woman didn't look left or right. Finster noticed that she carried more than her fair share of the luggage, and he wondered what their little drama was. Father and daughter? Husband and wife? Businessman and mistress? When the couple finally emerged from the makeshift bazaar, they were greeted by the village's only public transportation—a horse-drawn carriage and a trishaw. Despite the man emphatically telling the drivers no thanks, the drivers persevered. Finster secretly rooted for them. The boy with the carriage lashed his skeletal horse into rattled action, plodding along next to the couple, beckoning them to take a trot along the blazing beach. The old trishaw driver couldn't muster enough breath to pedal and speak at the same time. He just stared beseechingly at the couple's backs as he pumped laboriously in their wake. Finster knew the drivers had only thirty more yards to seal the deal before the couple reached the only possible destination—Motel Paradise, a queue of cinder-block bungalows with a thrumming generator and a hand-painted sign promising AIR CON.

"Mistah Finstah, what to do with the boxes, sah?"

Finster turned around just in time to see his shipment—half a dozen cardboard crates—flung out of the cargo hold and onto the puddled dock.

"Are you morons crazy?" he said, bending over to sniff for any breakage. Last month one of the boys had dropped a box on the pier and the smell had lingered for days. With all the other pungent odors around, you couldn't exactly distinguish any particular one, but still, walking along the wharf at night, when the sun wasn't out to cook up the rotting fish heads, Finster could swear he smelled his magic elixir and was filled with such profound longing, he almost believed the stuff worked.

Peeling back a cardboard flap, he could see the little vials shaken but unharmed in their cardboard cells.

"Stack them next to my warehouse. And be careful, for Christ's sake, or me tingktingk you not getting paid."

Then Finster slipped beneath the wharf, took another toke, and walked to the edge of the road to try to catch one last glimpse of the woman. The sun was flaring on the horizon, turning the corrugated tin village into glaring cubes on stilts of fire. Black clouds piled up overhead. Squinting into the frittering light, Finster could barely even see the motel, let alone any people around it. When he heard his boys laughing on the far end of the beach, he hurried toward his warehouse to make sure they weren't filching a vial or two.

The boys squatted beside the boxes, their cheeks ballooned with betel nut, their teeth stained the color of maraschino cherries. They were recent arrivals from a mountain kampung and wore the island equivalent of nouveau riche haute couture—baseball caps advertising products they'd never heard of, let alone could afford, and knockoff brand sneakers worn with the backs crushed flat and the laces flapping. One boy sprawled on the sand, lewdly pumping his hips while pretending to caress a penis as long and stiff as a baseball bat. When the others saw Finster, they leapt up and stood at mock attention.

"Sah, the boxes unloaded, sah," said the leader, a wild-haired boy of sixteen.

Finster took out his wallet. "Don't blow it all in one night," he said.

He paid them one American dollar apiece and a vial between them. The vials were worth more than money—the boys believed it gave them sexual power. Outside of their villages and the distant capital, the female pickings were slim. The Hindu and Muslim girls were all married off before puberty, the Chinese stuck to their own kind, and the natives who came down to the coast were snatched up by the missionaries. By thirteen, they wore hulking Mother Hubbards and carried around Bibles the size of cinder blocks.

After the boys left, Finster unlocked his warehouse, a tin Quonset hut at the hem of the jungle guarded by two squat, wrinkly-faced dogs. The dogs were sisters, most likely a mix of pye-dog and Chinese shar-pei, who seemed to resemble (particularly when Finster was high) W. H. Auden. He'd found them as pups, paid them in bones, and loved them to the point where he thought he was losing his mind. Dragging his boxes into the stifling hot hut, he stopped for a second to hold out his hands and let his girls kiss him like supplicants.

The warehouse had no electricity, so Finster worked by flashlight. He opened his boxes and started taking inventory. Between the heavy panting of the dogs and the insufferable heat, he felt as if he was working inside an engine.

The bulk of his stock was shipped from the Philippines. Finster had never met his counterpart in Manila, but he had a fair idea of the man's predilections. Each vial came wrapped in a wad of newsprint torn from Manila's raciest tabloids—blurred photos of bullet-riddled corpses, scantily clad "hostitutes," a Filipina maid stabbed to death by her Singaporean employer. Mostly, the articles were in Tagalog, but a few were in English, and in this piecemeal fashion, Finster got his news of the outside world. Pirates attack a city in

Borneo. Aquino threatens to cancel U.S. military base leases. Muslim insurgents start a holy war in Mindanao. Catholics are rioting on Flores because a Protestant refused to eat the body of Christ.

Tilting his head back against the tin wall, Finster dug out his roach and took another blast to blot out the news. Then he shut off the flashlight. The Quonset hut was a relic from World War II. Fifty-year-old bullet holes pocked the ceiling. When the moon was full, as it was tonight, light poured in like water through a colander. Unable to sit still for another second, Finster got up and herded his dogs outside. He liked them to prowl the beach at night to keep a blood-shot eye on things. With his Swiss army knife, he opened two cans of imported Alpo and emptied the horse meat into their bowls. While his girls ate noisily, a sound he found weirdly moving, he locked the warehouse and headed toward the motel. He just wanted to take a gander at what was going on, see if the woman was around.

The village, a pandemonium of tin shacks flanking ten dirt lanes, had already shut down. Even the chickens had disappeared. Finster walked along the beach, past the fishermen's huts, to the only paved road. It was paved with crushed coral and he had to stop now and again to dig an iridescent pink shard out of his rubber flip-flops. The motel stood in a grove of palms. Finster knew the Indian hotelier would have put the white couple up in his deluxe suite, the only room with a glass window, running water, and a toaster-size cooler. He crept around back, careful not to make a sound—not that anyone would hear him over the thrumming insects and knocking palms.

An oil drum stood under the couple's window. For a moment, Finster thought he saw it tilt. Inching closer, he did see it tilt. The missionary boy was perched on the barrel's rim, taking surreptitious peeks through the glass. Finster knew he was spying on the woman. He loathed the boy, but since he was the only other American around, they'd formed one of those uneasy alliances based entirely on homesickness. The boy had been sent here six months ago by the

Seventh-Day Adventists to convert any native who hadn't already been commandeered by the Mormons. But no one listened to the kid, let alone attended his weekly preach-o-thons. The Hindus laughed behind his back. The Muslims thought him mad. As far as Finster could tell, the entire doctrine of his church consisted of standing on a mountaintop and waiting for the world to end. Only when Finster was high, which was pretty much always these days, did he feel a fleeting sympathy for the boy. He'd call him Mr. Millennium and he'd let the kid show him his church's brochure—a coloring book Eden where lions lie down with lambs and every Melanesian looks like a young Harry Bellafonte or a smashing Lena Horne. With the right combination of pot, whiskey, and self-pity, Finster saw in those illustrations the world he thought he'd set sail for six years ago.

He picked up two coconuts and whacked them together. The loud clops, sounding like a bush pig stamping through the grove, sent the kid fleeing into the village. Finster hung back for a minute or two, then hoisted himself onto the barrel and took the kid's place. Through the pitted glass, he could see two shapes sleeping in separate beds. But that implied nothing. No one could sleep side by side in this heat. The man and the woman were naked. Under the mosquito net, details of the woman's body were blurry, but Finster could make out what he craved. She slept on her side, her legs folded, her cheek crushed against her shoulder. She didn't shave under her arms and Finster saw a cloud of red hair framed by the ghost of a bikini strap. Only one breast was visible. Finster had once read an article in a women's magazine that compared breast sizes and shapes to drinking glasses: the beer mug, the brandy snifter, the martini glass, and the ultimate size and shape—a wide-mouthed champagne glass. This was definitely a champagne glass.

Mashing his cheek to the window, Finster memorized the breast. Then, cupping the image in his addled mind, as carefully as a man might cup a handful of cherished water, he climbed off the barrel and walked to the beach. With a bamboo stick, he drew an outline of the woman in the sand, then lay down atop it. Without losing hold of the breast, he groped through his pocket for his roach and lit up. With every exhalation, he watched the smoke fly out of his mouth in the shape of his soul. When the roach finally dwindled to ash, the memory of the breast flitted away and a jolt of dire loneliness overtook him. He rolled onto his stomach and pressed his cheek against the warm sand. He could hear the land crabs' claws clicking like castanets and something lugubrious moving through the jungle. Sleep clotted his eyes. Then, on the brink of hallucinatory dreams, they came to him—the lions and lambs of Eden. The lions padded around him, the lambs nudged him with their cold noses. In a frenzy of love, they licked his eyes, ears, cheek, neck. He expected their breath to smell awful, but it smelled weirdly familiar—a waft of canned horse meat and something like a fever.

A frond crashed against the tin roof, or perhaps it was the dead Air Con finally clanging to life, or the thwacking palms, or her own blood banging in her ears. Helene opened her eyes, not quite sure where she was. A red paper arrow was Scotch-taped to the ceiling. Somehow she knew it pointed to Mecca, that she was somewhere in the East, that she'd traveled for days; the only certitude was a nagging sadness at the core of her being.

She sat up and hoisted the weight of her damp hair off her sweaty neck. She could hear the wind whizzing through the grove, but the air inside was thick and sticky as aspic. She climbed out of bed and tried to open the window. When it wouldn't budge, she wandered over to her husband's cot. He lay sheathed in sweat, snoring raggedly, his mouth open in sleeper's awe or dreamer's fright. One arm was flung toward her, the hand balled in a fist. He looked as if he'd been trying to punch his way out of the mosquito net.

She slipped on her robe, strode outside, and headed to the motel office, a cinder-block bunker under betel palms. She banged on the plank door. Through its gaping chinks, she could see a light flare and shudder, then bob forward.

The door cracked open and the Indian hotelier, a short, barrel-shaped man in a crumpled sarong, peered out, holding up a hurricane lamp. He had evidently been roused from sleep: His unshaven cheek still held pillow creases and his pomaded hair was a tornado of gray spikes.

"You promised you had air-conditioning, Mr. Khan. We need air-conditioning."

"Yes. No problem. We have air-conditioning."

"But it's not on. It's not working."

"Ah, that's because we have no electricity."

"Could you help me open our window at least?"

"I'm sorry, mem, the window is sealed to keep in the cold air."

"Please. There must be something you can do."

"I could see if there is gasoline in the generator."

"Thank you."

"*Sama-sama.*"

Helene returned to their room, tore off her robe, and sat down on the edge of her cot. For a moment, it felt as if the room had gotten hotter in her absence.

She fumbled in the dark for Thomas's cigarettes and lit one. In the closed space, the smoke clung to her. Her intuition generally let her know if he was all right, but the heat had left her stupefied, almost indifferent. She heard the Indian crank on the generator. It pinged, then chattered to life. She knew the air conditioner was finally on again because smoke, like blue ringlets, began drifting away from her.

She mashed out the cigarette, then lifted the net and caressed her husband's hand. The moment their skin touched, sweat began pooling. She lay down beside him, burrowing her face into the hollow of his arm. The combined heat from their bodies was insufferable, but she knew it wouldn't wake him. Often, now, he vanished into tranced sleep.

After a minute or two, wafts of tepid air reached them and she let herself drift into one of those light, fleeting slumbers; she felt blissfully unburdened, almost bouyant, as if she were rising up through fathoms of cool ocean. Then Thomas stirred and she opened her eyes and she was back in the stifling room with the red arrow and the pinging generator.

She sat up, accidentally awakening Thomas.

"I know it's cramped on your cot, darling, but I felt something crawling in my bed," she lied. As soon as she said it, she did feel something crawling on her legs. Whatever it was, its feet were as light as Styrofoam. It left footfalls of fire wherever it walked.

She began scratching her ankles, not like a woman alleviating the itches of a mosquito bite, but like a woman tearing off burning socks.

Thomas made her lie down, then ran his hands over her legs. "I don't feel anything," he said, "not even a bite."

"Maybe they're microscopic ants?"

"If you saw the size of the ants around here, I doubt you'd say that." He began rubbing her ankles and calves with exquisite pressure.

"Thomas, I swear there's something biting me."

He fetched the flashlight and inspected her skin with clinical precision.

"There's nothing on your legs, Helene, I promise you. It's probably just prickly heat. You always get it when you first arrive in the tropics. Do you want me to see if Mr. Khan has some jamu?"

Helene shook her head no. "I think they're real bites this time," she said quietly.

"Do you think you can go back to sleep now, darling?"

"I don't know. Maybe. I'd like to stay here with you."

He kissed the back of her dripping neck. "I don't think it's a good idea, Helene."

"We've made a horrible mistake coming here, haven't we?"

"Helene, we just got here." He pushed aside the netting, got up, and padded across the cement floor to the makeshift kitchenette—rusted sink, dripping faucet, kerosene stove. Squatting down, he found some empty tin cans under the sink and filled them with tap water. Returning to the cot, he asked Helene to stand up for a second, then hunkered down like a shoe salesman and set the cot's feet into the sloshing cans, like four tin boots. One can still wore its bright Spam label.

"You sleep here. There's not a bug, even a microscopic bug, in sight," he said. He straightened up and rested his chin on top of her head. He didn't embrace her. Even with the air conditioner chugging at full throttle, the heat was intolerable. "The ants won't cross the water. The net will keep out anything that flies." He touched her cheek; he didn't caress it, he simply pressed his hand against her skin. "I've got to sleep now, darling. I'm exhausted. You're perfectly safe. You should try to sleep, too."

Then he walked across the room, lay down on her bed, and pulled the net over him.

She watched him through its gauzy dimensions, and for a moment, he looked like a cut of meat draped in cheese cloth.

He fell asleep instantly, but she didn't. She lay unbearably alert in the dark, atop her bed, under her net, within her four tiny Spam can moats.

I am delighted you turned to me for my expertise and assistance. I happen to have a car with a promising license plate available for hire," Mr. Khan said. He slid out from behind his reception desk—an ancient school table shaggily stacked with papers. His pomaded gray hair now featured a ruler-straight part, and he was dressed in Western slacks. Helene noticed that his belt was a strip of electric tape. "Please, make yourselves comfortable."

It wasn't even nine A.M., and the cinder-block motel office had already reached kilnlike temperatures. The only chairs in sight were two airplane seats. The dents in the metal armrests lent them an air of salvaged disaster.

"I guess your brochure's advice about taking the ferry, as opposed to flying, wasn't such a bad idea after all," Thomas said, sitting down.

The Indian wagged his finger. "Very amusing, Mr. Strauss. No, the seats were taken from a movie prop. They shot the film a mile or so from here. It's about an airplane that crashes in the jungle and how we humans persevere. This village is on the map, Mr. Strauss."

Helene stood with her back to the fan, basking in its tepid breath. "Does the car have air-conditioning?" she asked.

"Yes, of course. No problem. It has air-conditioning." The Indian shuffled through his papers until he found a limp pink form bloated with carbons. "Is this business or holiday?"

"Holiday," Thomas said.

"May I ask what your itinerary is?"

"The capital, your beautiful beaches, the caves—"

"Ah, the Vatu caves! Did you know that many consider them to be the eighth wonder of the world?"

"Yes, we read that in your brochure. We'd also like to visit Kuantong and Minaphor. Is there a problem taking the car across the border?"

"We are a small island shared by three countries, Mr. Strauss. Our borders are more cultural than physical. We have had to learn to cooperate. There should be no problem at the border provided you have the correct documentation. This can be obtained in the capital, with the second copy of the pink form and a yellow one I will give to you in a minute. Please—" The Indian slipped Thomas his card. It read:

Mr. Khan, Proprietor / Motel Paradise
Safe-Deposit Boxes / Excellent Car Rental
Paradise Travel and Tours / Paradise Real Estate
Globe Imports and Exports
Problems solved here: free consultation

"I am also a tour guide, Mr. Strauss. I can show you superior sights not found in any tourist brochure. I have many interesting and amusing stories to tell." He rummaged through a drawer and hauled out a grubby sheath of envelopes. "These are testimonials from my pleased customers."

Helene turned around. "We want to be on our own," she said.

"I would not recommend it, mem."

"Why not?" Thomas asked.

"We are a new and very poor country, still making adjustments. The natives are very backward people, suspicious of foreigners. There is no danger, if that's what you're thinking, Mr. Strauss. Our government keeps all predicaments under control. The only dangerous thing is to miss the interesting and amusing stories I have to tell." He laughed, revealing an abundance of crimson teeth and gold inlays. "For example, did you know three thousand marines died on the beach where you landed? It was the Battle of Orang Puteh."

"I vaguely remember the name," Thomas said.

"I will tell you a story and if you like it, you can decide if my services are valuable. Pay or no pay, it is entirely up to you." He reached into his pocket and dug out a couple of betel nuts and pepper leaves. "Would you like to try betel, Mr. Strauss?"

"No, thanks," Thomas said.

"I can't blame you. It is a filthy habit. But what can I do? I am an addict." He rolled a jagged leaf around a nut, bit off one end, fished out a Ziploc sandwich bag of powdered limestone, and dipped the tip of the leaf into the acidic talc. Then he jammed lime, leaf, and nut between his teeth and gums and began chewing vigorously. A moment later, covering his mouth with his gemmed fingers, he spit, as discreetly as possible, a vermilion stream into a pewter spittoon. It pinged when it hit. "As you well know, last year was the fiftieth anniversary of your victory—our victory—over Japan. My country threw a big celebration and many of your marines, old men now, came to see the beach where they fought. Were you in the war, Mr. Strauss?"

"Which war?"

"Pacific?"

"Korea."

"Ah," he said, unleashing another red stream. "Your navy assigned young marines to reenact the landing, but the old men wouldn't hear of it. You saw our reef. It is treacherous. Some of the men were very frail and could barely get around on land, but they insisted on wading ashore themselves. To see these elderly gentlemen hold on to their dignity . . . well, I, for one, was very moved. When they finally reached the beach, most fell to their knees. Not from physical exhaustion, Mr. Strauss, but because they were weeping. What they saw in their mind's eye . . . who can imagine in these safe and prosperous times. The old natives say after Orang Puteh, the lagoon was red with blood for weeks. I was retained by Mr. Klingerman, a private, who had landed with the first wave. He claimed to have survived the shelling by hiding behind a rock for three days and nights. He requested my services to help him find the rock. I accepted no money. I have compassion. We looked everywhere. The landscape he remembered is not the palm-fringed beaches and majestic mountains that you see today in our tourist brochures. Our island had been bombed barren, first by the Japanese, then by you Americans. We searched for days. Is that the rock? Is that not the rock? All he had to go on was the memory of his bent body behind the rock. At last he thought he'd found it. He crouched down and contorted himself into the shape of the rock. Was it really his rock? This is a philosophical question I cannot answer. He asked if he could chip off a piece of the rock to take home with him. The exportation of any war relic, even a rock, is highly condemned by my government, and I regretfully explained our policy to Mr. Klingerman. After all, with no regulations, what would become of us? But, in the end, I broke down. Here was an old man, probably at the end of his days—"

Helene stepped away from the fan and abruptly left the room. The two men shifted in their seats and watched her.

"Did I say something to offend your daughter, Mr. Strauss?"

"My wife. No, the heat's just getting to her."

Their map showed a large amoeba-shaped island with only a few highways circumnavigating it, like a primitive circulatory system. Hundreds of islets dotted the sea around it. These were mostly uninhabitable limestone rocks capped by thorny jungle. The native creation myth, inscribed in a corner of the map, described the formation of the archipelago as a sexual act. A young girl, promised to a husband who was meagerly endowed, sought help from the women chiefs. They told her about a man with a fifty-foot penis. She traveled to the tip of the island and found him cracking coconuts with the shaft of his massive member. He said if she wanted him, she would have to swim out beyond the reef, where she would find his penis's tip. She found it and they made love with such ferocious abandon that she eventually broke apart into myriad islets that no man could ever inhabit.

At the top of the main island, isolated by the area's only navigable river and colored bright orange on the map, was Minaphor, an independent city-state. Its citizenry was mostly ethnic Chinese, descendants of poor peasants brought there by the British at the turn of the century to mine phosphate. One hundred years later, through discipline and sheer tenacity, they'd transformed the mostly swampy peninsula into a prosperous commercial hub, whose architectural style resembled a series of Southern California shopping malls, interspersed with skyscrapers. The president, a despot who'd long ago banned elections, ruled Minaphor with pitiless rigor. Political dissidents were hung, loitering was a jailable offense, even forgetting to flush a public toilet carried a fifty-dollar fine.

On the island's windward side, fortressed by rain-lashed mountains and colored mint green on the map, was Kuantong, an isolated Muslim enclave. Its natives had practiced Islam since the religion arrived in the fourteenth century with the spice trade. Only recently, with the infusion of fundamentalist immigrants, had these tolerant people been stirred into a frenzy of devotion—hijab was law, the mosque minarets screeched calls to prayer at deafening decibels, and Kuantongans now looked upon their Westernized island neighbors, sporting sneakers and baseball caps, with unmitigated disgust. Only three convoluted highways still penetrated Kuantong's borders. The rest of the roads were all Xed out.

On the island's leeward side, through which Thomas and Helene now drove, was Vanduu, a hodgepodge of cultures, a modern Tower of Babel. Aside from its cathedral-size caves, it was famous for its temples, its mosques, its churches, its *wats,* its poverty, its cargo cults, its psychosurgeries, its sex shows, but mostly, for its exquisite landscape, coral beaches, and viridescent sea. Which was what they had come for, or at least, what they told each other they had come for.

The map was open on Thomas's lap. Helene was driving, navigating down a bumpy back road, searching for the main highway to the capital. For the past hour and a half, they'd been following Mr. Khan's vague directions—"Turn north at the big rock that looks like a fist, veer west when you see Sleeping Dog Island"—until they were completely lost. On their left lay a gummy swamp, broken by charred tree stumps and flapping fruit bats. On their right hovered the jungle's skyline—irregular domes of tremulous foliage and spires of palm. Vines, with leaves the shape of Rorschach blots, tumbled out of the canopy.

They passed a rusty tin town—tin post office, tin church, tin grocery store, tinny puddles reflecting tin. The town's sign was rain-streaked and plastered on a corrugated tin fence. The letters looked as if they were undulating underwater.

Thomas glanced at the map and concluded that they probably were on the main highway.

Knots of women, balancing roped bundles of crooked sticks on their heads, and scrawny goats with yellow teeth and clanging bells padded along the shoulder.

The road looped by the coast again, revealing a sheen of viridian sea, then turned inland and huffed up the foothills where rice paddies, all angular grace and mirror-still, tiered the slopes. The silhouetted mountains above them were so flat and jagged, they looked as if they'd been cut out of green construction paper with a toenail scissors.

Helene noticed that Thomas was dozing off, and to keep him with her, she began pointing out sights to him, the little cultural incongruities he normally loved—a peasant wearing a straw hat sheathed in blue Saran Wrap like a slip-covered suburban lamp shade, a Muslim girl on a motorcycle, the fringe of her head scarf fluttering out of her helmet.

Thomas opened his eyes for a moment, then fell back to sleep, his body slumped against the seat belt, his head lolling, his jaw slack. The map slid off his knees. Without taking her eyes off the road, Helene reached over and tried to retrieve it, but her own seat belt held her in check. She sat back and lightly touched Thomas's face. It was halved by extremes: Where the sun struck it, it was burning; where the air conditioner blew, it was cold as a corpse. She nudged him back against the seat so that his head could rest on the cushion. Then she nudged him again, trying to wake him up. She said, "Sit up or you'll ruin your back," and actually tugged on his shirtsleeve. These were the moments she had come to dread, when frustration and responsibility reached the intensity of passion, when she felt more like his nurse than his lover.

The jungle closed in again and she suddenly had no idea where they were. She squinted out at the blowing hubbub of green, glare, shadow, and pulse.

"Thomas, wake up. You've been sleeping for over an hour." This wasn't true; he'd only toppled off about fifteen minutes before.

"Yes?" His voice sounded wide awake, but when she looked at him, he was fast asleep again.

The jungle gave way again and they were in farmland—taro? Cassava? Breadfruit? She couldn't recall what any of them looked like. She had a vague memory of a grade-school teacher saying, "And with God's blessing, the missionaries cut down the breadfruit and ended the savages' sloth," and her—six, maybe seven years old—envisioning a bearded missionary chopping down a tree laden with Wonder Bread loaves.

The road suddenly turned muddy and her right tires slid into a ditch and stuck. She gunned the motor, whirring the tires pointlessly. Thomas woke up. "It's about time," she said. She jerked the car into reverse, goosed the gas pedal, then crunched it into first gear and catapulted them free. Still accelerating, she flew over a hill and around a curve. Then she heard a thud, reminiscent of a slap on the face, but sickeningly louder, and her front tires clunked over a shape. She jabbed at the brakes, but the back tires clunked over the shape as well.

She skidded to a stop and stared in the rearview mirror.

Amid the coughed up dust, a pig lay on its side and lifted its head like a man with a piercing hangover.

Suddenly and stupidly, she ran out of the car, and Thomas ran after her.

The pig was still moving when they got to it, its rear hoof pedaling the air, its stomach heaving and rolling like an inner sea. Its face was smashed and dark with blood. Its blue eye, within pink lids, looked up at Helene, then Thomas. The eye was unbearably alert, insufferably conscious, and held all the bewilderment of a human eye.

Helene wanted to comfort the creature, but she was scared it would bite her.

"Thomas, please help it."

She heard rustling behind her, and seemingly from out of nowhere, a crowd began to gather. She glanced around and realized they were on the outskirts of another tin town.

"Is there a veterinarian nearby?" she asked.

No one moved. The men stared through her, leaning on muddy farm implements she couldn't recognize. She spoke slowly and loudly, enunciating each word as if addressing the deaf.

"Is there a vet-er-in-ar—" She stopped, realizing how ludicrous she sounded. "There must be a doctor somewhere? Please, I'll pay for a real doctor."

Thomas and one of the farmers hunkered down and knelt over the pig. The pig commenced squealing—a low-pitched whine that sounded like tape hiss.

"Could someone get a doctor please!"

A boy stepped out of the crowd and solidly kicked the pig's hind quarters with his sneaker.

"Stop it!" Helene said.

The pig grew quiet. The farmer put his hand on its chest.

"Babi dead," the farmer said.

Helene looked down. The pig's eye had become a glass marble, staring out of a blank socket.

Thomas wiped his face with his shirtsleeve, then slowly stood up, but the farmer remained where he was, jabbering at Thomas with constrained fury.

Helene couldn't understand a word of it.

"Helene, wait in the car," Thomas said.

A caravan of trucks, laden with logs as thick as freeway pillars, thundered past, followed by an ancient, swaying bus. The bus was top-heavy with luggage, and as it chugged by, Helene noticed it shudder to a near standstill so that the driver and passengers could rubberneck the dead pig and the dazed white couple and the fuming farmer. Then the bus varoomed loudly and sped up, only to slow down once again, coming to a bumpy stop a hundred yards up the road. For a couple of minutes, it idled in its own blue exhaust, before expelling a blond ponytailed young man and a bunch of cardboard crates.

Helene thought the man looked American. He wore rubber flip-flops and voluminous Hawaiian bathing trunks and had the knotty knees of an ex-surfer. After the bus rumbled off, he remained in the middle of the road, rubbing his eyes vehemently as if to screw them back into focus. Then he dragged his crates into the bushes and headed toward the melee.

The pig was blocking northbound traffic. Flies had formed a green aura around it.

Helene sat down on the car bumper, the rear bumper. The front one was speckled with blood.

Thomas was still trying to pacify the farmer, talking to him in a low, solicitous tone.

The young man elbowed his way through the small crowd, put his hand on Thomas's shoulder, then squatted down and addressed the farmer himself. With chameleonlike precision, he assumed the native posture—shoulders hunched, head bowed, eyes drifting. But he jabbered just as fervently as the farmer did.

In the stark sunlight, they looked, to Helene at least, like identical shadow puppets, ancient adversaries going about the motions of rage when they both seemed to know exactly how this fight would end.

Finally the young man turned to Thomas and asked for something, but Helene couldn't make out what it was. Thomas looked directly at her, then took out his wallet and gave the man money.

Slowly, methodically, almost seductively, the man folded the bill lengthwise and held it out to the farmer, but the farmer shook his head no. He pointed to his pig—smashed, fly-ridden—then put up his hands as if the young man held a weapon.

The young man rolled his eyes heavenward and sighed. "Me tingktingk you bright pela," he said. "Me tingktingk you take the fifty bucks and enjoy your pork chops."

The farmer looked disgusted, but he took the fifty anyhow. He jammed it into his leather pouch, then barked out orders, and a couple of teenage boys produced a rope, slung it around the pig's rear ankles, and began hauling it away. Helene watched in numb horror as the pig's bloody head clunked along the rocky ground.

Someone touched her arm and she reeled around. "Let's get out of here," Thomas said. The young man was standing beside him.

"Adam, my wife, Helene. Helene, Adam Finster. We're going to give him a lift to the capital, okay?"

Helene was still distracted by the pig; she could just make out the big gray shape being dragged into the village.

"Helene, where are the car keys?"

"What?"

"The keys."

"I think they're still in the ignition," she said.

The crowd hadn't broken up. The accident seemed to be the afternoon's entertainment. A group of men walked over to the car and squatted down to scrutinize the blood on the bumper.

"Let's go," Thomas said. "Now."

They got into the car, Thomas behind the wheel, Helene beside him, Finster in back. With jerky restraint, Thomas inched away from the men, then threw the car into first and weaved through the milling crowd. They stopped to pick up Finster's boxes, then sped on. A couple of boys chased them for a while, but Helene couldn't tell if it was in fun or fury.

Thomas squeezed her hand and asked if she was okay. When she nodded yes, he lit a cigarette and looked at Finster in the rearview mirror. "I didn't get a chance to thank you," he said.

"Hey, no problemo. Anything for my fellow Americans."

"The farmer seemed irate, Adam. Was fifty enough?"

"You kidding? Farmer John just won the Vanduu equivalent of the Publishers Clearing House Sweepstakes."

"He didn't look all that thrilled to me."

"Trust me, I work with these people, a good deal of his bluster was just an act to save face. You've got to understand, a lot of these old villages still run on pig economies. Pigs for power, pigs for prestige. With enough pigs, you can even buy yourself a wife."

Helene had no idea what the man was rattling on about, but whenever the word *pig* came up, she could see the eye revolve in its crushed socket and stare back at her.

"I knew a Vanduuan doctor, an orthopedic man, made a million in Honolulu setting the bones of surfers, but when he returned to Vanduu, he was nothing, squat. Why? Because he had not owned and killed pigs."

She pressed her temple against the window. Even with her eyes shut, the sun was so strong, sprockets of glare scrambled across her lids.

"If a pig—"

"Please! Do we have to talk about pigs!"

The silence that followed crackled like white noise.

For the next couple of miles, they drove beside a river with tin shacks mushrooming along its muddy banks. The closer they got to the capital, the more decrepit the houses became. The tin roofs and walls gave way to other materials—black tar paper and wooden crates branded with Chinese characters and scraps of electric-blue plastic. Here and there, a square white cinder-block apartment building, like an enormous cube of sugar, rose out of the squalor.

Helene glanced back at the young man. He looked genuinely

hurt and confused by her outburst. He kept stroking the infinitesimal smear of his blond mustache. His eyes were the cobalt blue of a milk of magnesia bottle. He couldn't have been older than thirty, if even that.

"Have you lived in Vanduu long, Finster?" she asked. For some reason, she couldn't bring herself to call him Adam.

"Six years and four months." He seemed depressed by his own answer. "I'm in the import-export biz," he added vaguely. "Vanduu's really not a bad place."

Out of the corner of her eye, she could see he was intently studying her. There was something slightly off about his surfer boy good looks: a hint of one too many indulgences.

"There's a lot of potential here," he went on. "Some big money's moving in. Especially from us."

"Who is 'us'?" Thomas asked.

"The good old U.S. of A. The Vanduuans joke that's why the sea around their island is so green, the whole place is afloat on American dollars."

"Why would the United States plunk money into Vanduu?"

"Things are iffy in the Philippines. Remember, we lost our main man there. No one knows what's going to happen next, if Cory's going to renew our military base leases or not. And Palau, the next island in line with a deep enough harbor, wants nothing to do with our nuclear ships. Unfortunately, we nuked a couple of their neighbors. And we're not exactly popular on Okinawa either. Hey, Vanduu is all we've got left."

"Somehow I can't imagine the Vanduuans greeting our warships with leis," Helene said.

"Well, there might be a few poison spears thrown, too," Finster said. He leaned forward and lowered his voice. "The sad fact is, if we flash enough dollars, everyone's happy to see us, Helene . . . at first."

On the left side of the road, a mountain of garbage rose, its western face catching the late afternoon light. Thin bodies weaved amid the refuse.

"They don't look too happy to me," Thomas said. "The dollars don't appear to be moving in here."

"They're scavenging for plastic and polyethylene. It's not exactly big bucks, but sometimes there's some pretty good finds to be had. I heard of a guy who actually collected an entire car in bits and pieces, then built his own taxi. He became a Vanduuan celebrity of sorts." Finster seemed relieved to be back on the subject of local lore again. "And there's always the furniture—you never know what you'll find. It's not well advertised, but Vanduu is famous for its nineteenth-century British Colonial antiques."

Helene looked out the window at the mounds of shredded plastic and crushed tin cans and burst out laughing, a little too shrilly.

The capital, six square miles of clotted traffic, tar-paper hovels, and fizzing neon, was beautiful for about five minutes every evening. The harbor, a sluggish gray bowl by day, turned into a pink and gold sea, and the main drag, a grimy eight-lane affair that girdled the water, vanished under a sheath of prismatic glare. Horns still blared, the traffic was still bumper to bumper, but the lumber trucks now looked as if they were laden with giant pastels and the gaseous buses spewed plumes of orange and even the buzzing pedicabs flashed by like jets of phosphorescence.

Finster guided them through a maze of back streets where onion-domed mosques, and hideous brick churches, and listing billboards advertising A&W root beer, Spam: a legitimate beef!, and *Rambo* in Hindi stuck out of a riot of shacks. Rheumy-eyed dogs and dust-covered urchins hawking Chiclets threaded their way through the stalled traffic. At the first major intersection, Finster instructed Thomas to turn right and park the car.

Without waiting for anyone else, Helene stepped out into the impossibly hot night. She took a deep breath, then lifted her hair off her damp neck and fanned her throat. In the periphery of her senses, she felt Finster's gaze slide over her as he climbed out of the backseat. While he and Thomas negotiated with a street kid to watch the car, she tried to catch Thomas's eye but failed. She wanted them to dump Finster as soon as they could, before Thomas invited the man to dinner out of his rigid sense of obligation. She wanted Thomas and her to be alone tonight. They needed to be alone. It was the reason they'd come on this trip. Besides, the kid's unflagging stare had begun to unnerve her.

She walked to the corner and leaned against a street lamp. They were on some sort of hotel strip. Dimly lit Chinese boardinghouses slouched beside ten-story modern shockers with blinking neon signs—THE CONTINENTAL, THE INTERNATIONAL, THE ORIENT. Doormen doubling as barkers were posted outside their garish lobbies.

"Come, come. We have Air Con. Plenty of vacancies."

"They all promise Air Con," Finster said, walking up behind her. "The trick is to know which one has twenty-four-hour electricity."

He led them down the block and into a mirrored lobby where the temperature was set at suspended animation. Flopping down on a big chair, luxuriating in the icy blast of relief, Helene suddenly didn't care if the three of them had to sleep in one bed as long as she didn't have to go back out into the heat again.

"They have two vacancies," Thomas said, kneeling down beside her. "One facing the street and one facing an alley. Finster said he'd take the one on the alley. Do you want to look at the front room before we register?"

"It has air-conditioning?"

"That's what the man said."

The elevator wasn't working and the stairwell, sealed behind glass doors, was stultifying. Before Thomas could stop her, Helene grabbed the heavier of their suitcases and began hauling it up the steps. Finster was still signing in at the front desk. He turned and curiously watched them.

Their room was on the second floor at the end of a musty green corridor. When Thomas unlocked the door, the room was throbbing with frigid pulses. An ancient air conditioner, with a Sanskrit logo, droned in the only window, a two-by-two sheet of mica-thin glass. The walls and ceiling were Pepto-Bismol pink. She stretched out on the double bed and closed her eyes. She could hear the rumble of traffic, the jimjam of horns. A bus rattled by, and she could actually feel the vibrations.

"Come lie down next to me, Thomas, and rest for a while."

"I can't. I promised to help Finster with his boxes."

"You're not going to lift anything heavy in this heat, are you?"

"Helene, please, I'm not going to lift anything heavy. I'm just going to guard the boxes while Finster and the doorman get them into the lobby. He asked if we could all go out on the town tonight."

"I wanted us to be alone tonight."

"We're going to be alone for the next month, Helene. The kid helped us out. What would you like me to do?"

"I'd like you to tell him that you want to be alone with your wife on the second night of your vacation." She rolled over and faced the pink wall. A dead mosquito lay squashed in a shoe mark.

"Helene, I already said we would go. We'll make it an early evening, okay?" Thomas leaned over and kissed her on the neck. "Besides, he's promised to show us the real Vanduu."

"I don't know if I can bear to see the real Vanduu," Helene said.

According to Finster, the capital was famous for its snake temple, its butterfly temple, its colonial antiques, its politics by murder, and its sex shows. The snake and butterfly temples closed at dusk, the antiques were peddled in private, the murders took place in secret, so Finster led them through the tourist district to the girlie bars. He tried to explain that most of the bars doubled as restaurants and karaoke clubs and that the girls were really very nice.

The faded publicity posters, thumbtacked under moldy glass and lit by hissing fluorescents, read "Fresh from Pattaya and Bangkok," "Wildest Show East of Manila," "Poppers, Best Showgirls in Vanduu," "Emmanuelle Look-a-likes," and Helene had the dire feeling that these photographs were taken years ago, that the clownishly made-up girls with their stand-up breasts and lacquered high heels had thickened into middle-aged women, that the young transvestite boys with their teased manes and Kewpie-doll lips had grown coarse beards that no makeup could ever cover.

Thomas whispered into her ear, "My God, this looks depressing."

"As long as they serve food and have air-conditioning, I'll watch elephants fuck."

The club that Finster finally decided upon, after dragging them up and down, up and down the traffic-clotted, gimcrack streets, was a tame affair, and Helene knew at once that Finster had shuffled through his dirty deck to find the least offensive card; the poor boy was actually trying to impress them.

Disco lights were popping as they walked in. A throng of Japanese tourists doing a robotic version of the Pony shook the dance floor. Mirrored balls orbited overhead. Finster led them to a table in the back and they all squeezed in. When Helene's eyes finally adjusted to the jabbing lights, she looked around and realized that the walls were wallpapered with the skins of mattresses. She could actually read the brand names—Beautyrest, Sleepytime, Posturepedic. An imp-size man in polyester bell-bottoms gingerly approached the table and asked Thomas to dance.

"Please do consider," he said politely.

Thomas looked querulously at Finster.

"Hey, it's not a gay thing," Finster said. "Most of these guys come over from Kuantong to whoop it up—you know, get blottoed on forbidden whiskey and ogle the girls. They're strict Muslims, though, so they draw the line at asking strange women to dance."

Thomas turned to the man. "I'm flattered," he shouted over a thudding rendition of "Raindrops Keep Falling on My Head," "but I'm afraid I'm too tall for you."

"No disco boogie?"

"Sorry," Thomas said, "no disco boogie tonight."

The man bowed deeply, then disappeared into the packed dance floor.

A Thai bar girl in white Nancy Sinatra boots ambled over and put some peanuts on the table. Helene ravenously devoured them. "God, I'm famished. May we see some menus, please?" she said.

"It's not exactly a menu kind of place," Finster explained. He signaled the girl and whispered in her ear. "I ordered you the house special," he told Helene. "It's really pretty good."

Helene looked around at the mishmash of decor, part suburban disco, part mattress store, part theme park, and couldn't imagine what the house special might be.

When the music ceased and the dancers quit, all the bar girls put down their trays and clapped to beat the band.

"They certainly are enthusiastic," Thomas said.

"They're fined five bucks a pop if they don't clap," Finster said.

Two speakers the size of coffins were pushed onto the stage, and the emcee, a Filipino version of Bert Parks, sauntered out in cowboy boots and grinned at the audience. "Howdy, folks," he said in a poor imitation of a Texas drawl. "Welcome to Club A-Go-Go. We are proud to present for you a wild, wild floor show tonight!"

The audience hooted and clapped.

"Why is he dressed like a cowboy?" Thomas asked. "Is there a theme to this place I'm not getting?"

"America," Finster said.

The emcee flapped his hands, signaling the audience to quiet down. "Tonight we offer for your delight our beautiful Filipina girls, toasts of Manila!" He whipped out a red-and-white-checkered bandanna and dramatically mopped his brow as if the mere mention of the girls made him break out in a cold sweat. "And, of course, our famous Bad Boys. Give all a big hand."

Over the raucous clapping, Helene could hear sporadic "Yee-haws" and whistles.

Then "Tie a Yellow Ribbon 'Round the Old Oak Tree" boomed over the speakers and a half dozen girls filed out. They were not dressed like cowgirls. They were dressed like Pocahontas in buckskin vests and beaded miniskirts. They looked sixteen years old, seventeen tops. For a full minute, they stood stock-still in coy terror while the music rumbled out of the shimmying speakers. Then, one by one, they hurried through their routine, a cross between a pow-wow dance and Miss America's runway walk.

When the song ended, the girls practically ran off the stage and the "Bad Boys" strode on, four Asian transvestites in chintz and flounce. They locked arms and, with bold operatic gestures, lip-synced to "The Way We Were." Since English wasn't their first language, their coral-red lips never quite synced up with the lyrics: They just opened and closed, opened and closed, like fish breathing.

When the girls returned, sporting leopard bikinis and red stilettos, the audience stamped their feet and hooted. To a disco version of the theme song for *Charlie's Angels,* the girls walked back and forth, back and forth, more in nervous strides than sultry pivots, as if they'd just missed the last bus home from the beach and were stranded.

Next, the boys minced out, also sporting bikinis, but theirs were far skimpier than the girls'. While they danced what appeared to be a hora to "Jambalaya," one of the boys kept letting his strap fall down. He must have spent his life savings on hormone treatments because a tiny, perfectly realized breast popped out. He wantonly squeezed it.

The audience tittered and clapped.

Finally, the girls came out in traditional G-strings. Helene noticed a few extra women among them. As "Like a Virgin" thumped through the floorboards, the girls attempted to bump and grind, but they jiggled rather than bumped, and galumphed rather than ground. Only one stood out. She was far older than the others, and acne-scarred, and plump, but she knew exactly what she was doing. Helene noted, with the cold appraisal of an old pro herself, just how good the woman was. In perfect time to the music, her breasts shimmied like sunlight on spinning hubcaps. Her eyes didn't drift coyly downward, or seductively upward: They held neither pleasure nor displeasure. Her indifference was transcendent, vast, complete. Here was sexuality without human frailty, and it was stunning. Suddenly, it was twelve years ago and Helene was back onstage and she knew, with absolute clarity, exactly what that power felt like.

She turned to Thomas. He was leaning on his elbow, watching the girls with a look of abject defeat, and the cruel reality of his illness broke her spell. She jerked back her chair, got up, and went into the bathroom. She leaned over the sink and splashed tepid water on her face, throat, and neck.

The attendant, an elderly Melanesian woman in a filthy T-shirt that said *Chanel,* sidled up behind her and started massaging her shoulders.

"What the hell are you doing?"

"Would you like a massage? Only fifty American cents."

Helene handed the woman whatever change she had in her pocket and left. When she returned to the table, a bowl of murky noodle broth sat waiting for her. She could see chunks of gelatinous canned chicken floating beneath the surface. The boys were back onstage, draped in flowered material that could have come from her grandmother's sewing chest. They were lip-syncing to "We Are the World."

"Let's get out of here, Thomas. I don't think I can take the grand finale."

Finster reeled around. "But you haven't tasted the house special yet."

"I'll pass."

"I'll go with you," he said, starting to rise.

"Stay, Adam," Thomas said. "Enjoy yourself. Have another drink. Helene and I are exhausted. We're going back to the hotel." He slid some money under Finster's sticky beer mug, and he and Helene left the bar.

They walked arm in arm through the streets, past vinyl-clad, spike-heeled girls slouched against walls, and stumbling, tanked sailors, and crumpled forms of indeterminate sex sleeping in doorways.

Pedicabs buzzed by like insects.

When they got back to the hotel, their room was entombed in musty heat.

"Who the hell turned off the air conditioner?" Helene said, jabbing at the ancient buttons until the contraption gurgled, then hummed.

Thomas flopped down onto the bed and Helene joined him, laying her head on his chest.

"That was the most depressing strip show I've ever seen," he said. He lifted her hair off her sweaty neck and gently blew. "And as you know, I've seen my share."

"Do you remember the boys' outfits, the ones in the last act? I think the flowered capes were made out of the same material my grandmother used for her living-room drapes."

Thomas laughed. Helene unbuttoned his shirt and caressed his chest and stomach, casually, so as not to seem too assertive.

"And the red stilettos. I swear I owned the same pair in 1983."

"I believe you did," he said, smiling.

She skimmed her lips across the coils of his gray chest hair, then hunkered down at the bottom of the bed and undid his belt, button, and zipper. Reaching inside, she pulled out his penis as gently as you might release a child's arm stuck in a coat sleeve. To keep up the semblance of lightness and spontaneity, she didn't suck it, she simply graced it with her lips. When she felt Thomas stir, so slightly it might have been from the vibrations of traffic, she lowered her mouth over it and began moving up and down. Because he wasn't erect, her concentration was divided—motion and slippage, action and stasis, risk and rebuke. To keep herself from thinking, she worked with steadfast concentration on the penis, giving little thought to the man behind it, as one might become fixated on polishing a lamp base when the whole room needs cleaning.

Then she heard a sob, no louder than a hiccup, and stopped. Pressing her brow against his thigh, she listened for another, but there wasn't one.

Outside, tires hissed, gears shrieked, buses thundered by.

A subterranean sadness tugged her under. She steeled herself, then crawled up the concave mattress to her husband.

In the dim light, his face looked like the memory of a face—a smudge of jaw, a blur of cheek.

"I am so sorry, Helene," he said. "I—"

"It's all right." She dug her face into the hollow of his arm, feeling a desire for him that seemed almost palpable. "I'm not in the mood either," she lied.

"Helene, it's never going to get better. Ever. You understand that."

She couldn't tell if it was a question or not. She slammed her eyes shut and wouldn't answer him.

"You don't have to stay with me. It's only going to get worse from here on in. You're still young. You can—"

She let the din of traffic blot out his voice. She didn't want to talk about it tonight. Matter of fact, she never wanted to discuss it again. Burrowing herself against his thin body, she tried to will herself to sleep, but she couldn't shirk off irksome consciousness with all its careening doubts.

After a couple of minutes, she sensed Thomas drift off, felt the grip of his sleep-laden arms slacken. Crawling out from under the dead weight of them, she sat up and reached for the light. She knew the light wouldn't wake him. Nothing woke him these days.

He was lying on his side, snoring softly, his jaw slack, his belt undone, his shirt pulled up, his pants open, his penis limp against his thin white thigh.

She looked at this man whom she deeply loved—old, exposed, frail—this man whom she'd just dragged halfway around the world to this Pepto-Bismol–pink hotel room with its forty-watt bulb, and it finally hit her with a visceral force she could no longer evade, that what Thomas had said *was* true, that it wasn't going to get better, that he could only get sicker, and they could get on more planes and ferries, they could rack up more miles, they could go next to Borneo or India or his beloved Amazon, but they simply couldn't outrun his illness.

He moaned and rolled over. The totality with which sleep took him these days, leaving all the indignities of his age and infirmity revealed, broke her heart. She pulled down his shirt, unlaced his shoes, and covered him with a sheet.

She got up and walked over to the window. Cupping her eye to the glass, she looked down at the ceaseless cones of headlights, the garish neon signs, the whole foreign sprawl of tin and pedicabs. Then she looked back at Thomas—oblivous, lost—and thought, If I don't have a drink, I'm going to be up all night, and if I spend another night watching him sleep, I'm going to go mad.

She slipped on her sandals and walked down to the hotel bar.

After the fluorescent stairwell, and the hideously bright lobby, the bar, a cavernous alcove in the back of the building, was impenetrably dark, save for glints of red—red vinyl booths, red tiles, red bar stools capped with little red mushroom seats.

She sat down on one and ordered a scotch. As soon as it came, she gulped it down and ordered another.

"You really shouldn't be in here alone, Helene." Finster had come up behind her.

"I thought you were staying for Club A-Go-Go's grand finale."

"Hey, seen one grand finale, seen them all." He lowered his voice. "Really, Helene, Vanduu City can be weird at night, you shouldn't be in here alone. You're the only white woman in the hotel."

"From what I could see tonight, Finster, it looks like I'm the only American woman in Vanduu."

"Well," he said, smiling, "we're not yet on the Princess Cruise circuit. Mind if I join you?"

She shrugged, then gestured to the stool beside her. She wanted to be alone and she didn't want to be alone.

"Can I get you another?"

"Let me finish this one first."

"Sorry about the show tonight. I guess it was a little more Vanduu than Vegas."

"It certainly was original."

"Tom joining you for a nightcap?"

She took a long sip. "He's not feeling well. He's gone to bed." She immediately regretted having said that: It felt like betrayal.

"Anything I can do? I know a good Vanduuan doctor."

"That's kind of you, Finster, but I'm sure he'll be fine." She felt like crying; she turned away and stared into the bar. A succession of hulking shapes teetered on stools. She could just make out, in one booth, a Vanduuan girl's frizzy head and the hairy white hand that stroked it. "Actually," she said, forcing a smile, "you can get me another drink."

"Scotch and soda?"

"You can skip the soda."

He gave her a curious look, then signaled the bartender.

"So tell me, Helene, what's a nice girl like you doing in a place like this?"

"You chose the hotel, Finster."

"I meant in Vanduu, Helene."

"Fun in the sun." She closed her eyes and took another long sip.

"Helene, you okay?"

"Fine, Finster, I'm just not feeling talkative tonight."

"Hey, if you want me to leave, I'll leave. I just don't think you should be in here alone."

"I don't want you to leave, Finster. Talk to me. Tell me *all* about life in paradise."

He studied her for a moment (she could see he wasn't sure if she was mocking him or not), then began telling her about Vanduu, but she wasn't listening. She was back in the room with Thomas, but she didn't want to be in that pink room with Thomas: She'd prefer to be in this garnet-red bar, listening to this handsome stranger's breathy version of paradise. Finster leaned closer, resting his arm on the back of her stool, his hand grazing her shoulder blade. She could have moved, but she didn't move.

"So, in the myth, Helene, the girl goes to the tip of the island and finds the man with the . . . well, how should I put it, the very gifted attribute."

"Lucky girl."

"Actually, it's a sad story. She dies the instant her love is consummated."

"There are worse ways to go," Helene said. She was more than a little drunk.

"I'm afraid it's not exactly a case of experiencing nirvana, then peacefully fading away, Helene. Their sex was so . . . *so rigorous,* . . . and his contribution so . . . *enormous,* she broke apart. The islanders believe that Vanduu is made up of her body parts. If you're born in Ngliik, where her head landed, you're supposed to be smart and talkative. If you're born in Bintan, where her stomach fell, you're rumored to eat seven times a day."

"And what part of her anatomy are we standing on here?"

Finster inclined his head and grinned. "Actually, they say that's why sex shows flourish in Vanduu City."

Helene laughed, then finished her drink. Finster had not moved his hand, save to wedge it a little tighter between the stool's vinyl back and her scapula.

"Another round?"

"I don't know."

"It's not even midnight, Helene."

She glanced at her watch: The gesture was perfunctory. She knew if she had one more drink, she'd cross that dubious line between cognizance and blurry consequence. "All right. One last round," she said.

The bar's only light fixture, a brassy, four-bulb affair, suddenly dimmed, brightened, flickered, then died. The room became so black that Helene actually saw afterimages. When she turned her head to find Finster, the rim of her glass cartwheeled across her vision. She couldn't exactly find Finster, but she could feel his hand. It now encircled her shoulder in a gesture more exploratory than protective.

"What the hell is going on?" she asked.

"Power outage. Happens all the time. The islanders call it a Vanduuan eclipse."

"I thought you said this hotel has twenty-four-hour electricity."

"They have a generator, Helene, they may not have fuel. Hang on a minute, the power sometimes comes back on."

She blinked into the blackness for what seemed like an interminable minute. Somewhere in the periphery of her besotted mind, she realized that Thomas was alone in that hideous pink room, in absolute darkness, without air-conditioning.

"I've got to get back to Thomas," she said.

"Give it another sec, Helene. The power's finicky; it could still snap on."

"I've got to go *now,* Finster." She shrugged his hand off her shoulder, slid off her stool, and began groping her way along the sticky edge of the bar. She bumped into what felt like a solid, sweaty punching bag. The bag swore at her in Vanduuan.

"Helene, wait." Finster caught up with her. "You can't just stumble around in the darkness." He lowered his voice. "It's not exactly safe to wander around by yourself during a blackout."

Wrapping his arm around her shoulder again, he clicked on a tiny flashlight attached to his key ring. The flashlight was pink and plastic and molded into the shape of a shrunken Occidental head. Light leaked out of its eye sockets and nostrils. A weak beam shot out of its gaping mouth.

"You couldn't find a less offensive flashlight, Finster?"

"I'm afraid it's the only kind you can buy in Vanduu that works." He shone it up at his face, replicating the shrunken head's look of boiled terror, and Helene was just drunk enough to laugh.

They began stumbling through the bar, illuminating the hulking shapes' sweaty visages. In the lobby, they almost crashed into a chair where a red-faced European and a Vanduuan girl's fishnetted thigh wavered in their paltry glow. Finster found the staircase and they staggered up.

He was holding her very protectively, more than protectively, and she was leaning into him. She wondered if she was quite as drunk as she was acting, or maybe she was even more drunk than she knew. She couldn't tell. At the top of the steps, Finster said, "You can still change your mind about that nightcap, Helene. I keep a bottle in my room."

Then he leaned over and kissed her. His breath smelled of whiskey and smoke and something weirdly reminiscent of childhood, like graham crackers. His lips had absurdly landed on her nose, and he had to tilt her head back to cover her mouth. He tried to maneuver his tongue between her teeth, but she kept her teeth locked. She could have pushed him off at this point, but to do so would have only created more of a scene than this little indiscretion warranted.

Without a semblance of encouragement or discouragement, she allowed him to finish his awkward kiss, then stepped back.

"Would you like that drink, Helene?" His voice was touchingly hoarse.

"I think we've both had enough, Finster."

"You sure?"

"Drop it, Adam. I've got to get back to Thomas."

She turned and headed into the darkness, feeling her way along the corridor's clammy walls, terrified of what might be crawling on them.

He caught up with her, gingerly took her elbow, and escorted her to her door. He held up the light while she rummaged through her purse for the keys.

"Helene?"

"What?"

"You're not angry, are you?"

"I'm drunk. We're both drunk."

"Would you like to keep the flashlight? You never know when the power's coming back on."

She didn't want to have to explain the flashlight to Thomas.

"I'll be fine. Could you just shine it at the door so I can get my key in the lock?"

She fumbled with her keys while he held the beam on the door, but now and again, the beam wavered. She knew he was using it to scrutinize her. She hated herself for having encouraged this boy, for having spent the evening flirting with him in that sleazy bar, but mostly, she hated herself for so desperately needing to do it.

She opened the door and quickly closed it behind her.

The room had already heated up. It felt as stultifying and airless as a crypt.

"Thomas?" she called, knowing full well he wouldn't answer. Once he'd toppled into sleep there was no calling him back.

She began groping her way through the dark toward their bed. When her shins bumped into its lumpy presence, she got undressed and laid down. With exquisite delicacy, she reached over and brushed the hair off his brow, then lifted his shirt and caressed his back and shoulders. He lay facing the wall. His skin still retained a chill from the air conditioner. His body temperature actually seemed colder than the room's. Pressing herself against him, she felt as if she were lying next to death.

It had been Helene's idea to come here. When Thomas's second round of radiation (what Thomas and Helene had disparagingly referred to as "the second scourge") was finally over, and his oncologists had reluctantly given their approval for him to travel again, Helene had become obsessed with the idea of their traveling. She tried to convince herself that travel was exactly what Thomas needed, but, in truth, she didn't think that either of them could handle one more day in their apartment with its interminable reminders: the Chinese herbs bought in a cold panic, the prostate cancer books with their brave and brainless titles, the countless prescription bottles with their cheery turquoise and taupe, canary and lime, pink and coral pills.

She'd scoured the Internet and written to every potential tourist bureau in the far-flung tropics. She knew exactly the kind of place she was looking for. It had to be an equatorial country that Thomas had never done field research in, preferably a country he'd never visited. It had to have a viable culture, preferably a polytheist culture, or at least one that would intrigue Thomas. It had to have great physical beauty, and restful beaches, and just enough of an infrastructure so as not to tax him when they traveled. But, above all, it had to have no resorts and few tourists, or Thomas would feel he was being conscripted into retirement, or worse.

When Mr. Khan's handmade brochure arrived amid the glut of

glossy government tourist pamphlets, Thomas had seemed charmed by its out-of-proportion ambitions: the ten-page mimeographed history of Vanduu, the language lesson with its hearty assurance "If Vanduuan proves too impossible, English is our number-two language!," the cockeyed English itself—"a splendific island," "a boogie-on-down capital"—but mostly by the hand-painted photograph of Mr. Khan grinning with black teeth and pointing up at his dinky cinder-block motel as if it were the Ritz. Just the fact that Thomas showed an interest in anything even remotely resembling their future was enough for Helene to fixate on Vanduu.

Somehow she'd gotten it into her head that if she brought him back to the tropics, to a place at least as remote as his Amazon, the sheer newness, the unrelenting beauty, the intrigue of an unprobed culture, the mere fact of their traveling together again, would make him, if not exactly well, at least himself; and Thomas hadn't had the heart to tell her that if he never saw another sad tropics, that if he never encountered another tin roof or undernourished dog or polytheist culture, it would be too soon; that what she hoped for would never happen, least of all in the lassitude of the equator; and that what he really wanted, in the best-case scenario, was to be allowed to grow old, and in the worst, to die at home.

He lay propped on his elbow watching her sleep in a white-hot bar of early-morning light. Even in sleep, when everyone else's face empties out like a sack, hers remained hard, fixed, alert. The temperature in the room was stifling, but he didn't dare move: The slightest jar of the mattress often woke her, and he didn't think he could bear to face her just yet. These days, her first few seconds of wakefulness were permeated with such sadness that he felt compelled to act cheery and buoyant, full of promise and health, and he simply didn't have the energy for it any longer. He watched her eyes, under papery lids, rolling after dreams he preferred not to know about. He'd been married twice before. His first wife had died of polio while he was off at war, a reversal of fortune that left him bitter and dazed. His second marriage had been a slam-bang disaster, giving him two children he loved but didn't like. Only at fifty-four, when his hair was gray, and his life's work seemed beside the point, and his renown was a burden rather than a pleasure, did he fall in love for the first time.

Helene had been a preposterous choice for a wife, as his colleagues and his grown children had made abundantly clear. But it really hadn't been a question of choice. They met while he was doing a comparative field study on the influence of technology on erotic dances in preindustrial and postindustrial societies. The study was a ruse: At this point in his life, he was spiraling out of control. After three weeks of deafening music and beer-splashed tables in countless strip clubs, he honestly couldn't tell the difference between his motivations for haunting these dives and those of the other glassy-eyed men in the audience. From the stage of the Kitty Club in Hollywood, Helene had spotted him interviewing her fellow dancers, approached him, and with a twenty-two-year-old's brazen audacity, offered to be his official guide to this underworld if he would pay her way out of this hole. He'd been so intrigued by the naive bravado of her proposal, and by her stunning good looks, that he took her with him on the rest of the study, all the way down to Brazil, and when it was over, brought her back to live with him in New York.

A wise girl, Helene quickly shed the coral lipstick and the spangled miniskirts, and learned to don the demure black wardrobe of a New York intellectual's mistress, but there were always the telltale signs of her class—a cheap bracelet, a loud laugh, a run in a stocking squelched by a dollop of nail polish. In those first years, whenever they traveled together to do field research, it was she, not he, who could turn a dry anthropological interview into a bawdy night of jokes, during which secrets Thomas would never have gotten otherwise were revealed. She was exceptionally good at fieldwork because she had no preconceived ideas about it. She read all the books he gave her, but she simply refused to accept the concept of the "other," and that refusal to cleave the world into "Them" and "us," made him respect her even more. Often, after a day's work together, he'd feel such inexplicable tenderness for this child that it actually scared him. Whatever he'd enjoyed before with his wives and his mistresses was many things—pleasure, diversion, passion—but not love. Only Helene, with her exhausting youth and stubborn bravado and cheap bracelets, had moved him. Even now, after twelve years of marriage, he still felt such compassion for this life that it amazed him.

He carefully slid out of bed, brushed aside the mosquito netting, then crept past her ever-alert head and went into the bathroom. He stood over the toilet bowl. A diagram illustrating how to use a Western toilet was laminated to the top of the tank. A stick figure squatting on the seat was Xed out; another facing the bowl, like a man staring into an abyss, was given the circle of approval. Thomas turned around and sat down. With no one looking, he preferred to sit like a woman these days; his flow was so piddling and erratic, it only disheartened him to watch it. He relieved himself with pleasurable urgency, knowing how hard he'd worked for even this much control.

When he returned to the room, Helene was sprawled diagonally across the bed, snoring softly, her arms flung over her eyes, her hair damp with sweat.

He scribbled her a note saying that he was going for a walk, got dressed, and headed down to the lobby. Stopping by the front desk, he asked when the electricity was coming back on. A toothless bellhop whose sunken chin barely reached the top of the Formica counter gave him a lost, placating, totally inconclusive smile.

Lighting a cigarette, Thomas stepped out into the rumble and glare of Vanduu. For a fraction of a second, with such intensity that it felt like a physical sensation, he was somewhere else, it was a long time ago. Sâo Paulo? Macapá? Between the bouncing light and the suffocating heat and the hefty wafts of diesel fumes, as evocative as any ex-lover's perfume, he wasn't sure. Then the gust of memory faded, and Vanduu, with its slapdash charm, reassembled before him. He started walking toward the harbor. Wherever he was in the world, he always walked toward the water.

It was before rush hour, if Vanduu even had a rush hour, and the Indian shopkeepers were cranking up their iron gates, revealing the most improbable combinations of wares: Xerox and Juicy Meats / Dentist and Hairdresser / Massage and Sweets / Fish and Auto Supplies. Squeezed into gaps between the dark, dusty shops crouched the money-changer shacks, dozens of them, all with exactly the same rates. The street vendors were also setting up, demarcating their spots on the bare, sizzling sidewalk with slabs of cardboard.

He passed a temple with a big brass Buddha and a mosque where white-clad men, crouched in prayer, looked like sacks of flour.

One street was filled with stalls of durian, a big armored fruit, a medieval-looking pineapple that smelled like the hamper of a hardworking athlete.

A tinny radio blared from an open window where a woman's slender arm was hanging up birdcages. A couple of urchins, sporting T-shirts that said *Rambo,* tried to sell him bags of steamed peanuts, and a man on a skateboard, paralyzed as if he'd been flash-frozen in the shape of a man in an easy chair, tried to hawk him lottery tickets. The sign around the man's neck read A WINNER NEVER QUITS, A QUITTER NEVER WINS!

Thomas bought two tickets, then gave them to the boys and walked toward the Philippine Sea. Gulls were wheeling over the pewter swells. Fishing boats, with dragons carved out of their prows, bobbed amid the foam. An eight-lane highway of whizzing traffic separated him from the sea's rampart, and Thomas couldn't quite get himself to cross it. He turned around and walked back into Vanduu, through a smoky, crowded alley where a tiny fire was burning in a makeshift shrine. The shrine was flanked by cheap porcelain figurines, not unlike the tchotchkes that had filled his grandmother's living room. Squatting beside the shrine, a Chinese boy was hawking paper toys—flimsy houses and cars and play money. The toys were scattered on a filthy blanket like a poorly planned paper town. An old Chinese man, standing next to Thomas, bent down, and with tender, excruciating deliberation, picked and purchased a house with a TV antenna clumsily penciled on its roof. The house looked as if it had been scissored and glued together by a kindergarten class. Holding the house in his cupped hands, the old man approached the shrine and bowed.

Thomas asked a passerby, a chunky, flat-headed Vanduuan in a cheap black business suit, what was going on.

"It is a heathen ceremony," the man said. "The Chinaman is sending things to his relatives in the spirit world, but Jesus says in heaven we will not be in want of material things."

As soon as the Vanduuan left, an old Chinese woman spit in the wake of his clopping black shoes. "It house with TV set for dead wife," she whispered to Thomas. Her face looked as if it were made out of bark. She was holding a paper car.

The old man set the house on the coals. He didn't flinch from the heat. The paper floor turned soot brown, then bright crimson, then gas-flame blue. And the little walls shook—no, trembled. Then a long lavender-tipped flame consumed the roof and the house took off with a formidable explosion, bursting into whirling cinders and raining ash. The ash rained on the porcelain figurines, but the cinders spiraled up into the sky. Only the burning floor remained. Then, in a puff of incandescence, it, too, was gone. The old man clapped three times, bowed three times, and walked away.

The sheer beauty of the ceremony almost made Thomas want to write again, but the impulse passed, like a momentary crick in an unused muscle, and he walked back to the hotel.

When he opened the lobby doors, a blast of frigid air stunned him, and once again, for a fraction of a second, he lost his place on the globe. He was walking into the ice-cold lobby of the Hilton in Brasilia; an anthropologist colleague, a man too old to do fieldwork, waved to him from a bar stool. Then Thomas blinked and the colleague transmogrified into the toothless Vanduuan bellhop, and the dinky, gaudy lobby with its gilt-flecked mirrors closed in on him. The electricity was back on. A buffet breakfast was stewing in steel trays above Sterno flames. Wagner was playing over the PA system.

Thomas headed upstairs and unlocked their door. Another shock of cold air greeted him. Helene was sitting up in bed, sipping a cup of black coffee. A shoe-shaped, half-eaten roll sat on the night table.

"Is that marching music?" she asked incredulously.

"Wagner in all his glory. They're playing him over the PA."

"Is it a national holiday?"

"It's some sort of Chinese Day of the Dead, but I doubt the Wagner's in homage to the Chinese."

He sat down on the edge of the bed and tucked a wisp of her sleep-crimped hair behind her ear. "Did you sleep okay?"

She shrugged. "I woke up with a splitting headache." She stared into her tar-black coffee, then took another sip. "It's probably the heat," she added.

"Did you take aspirin?"

She nodded.

"When did the power come back on?"

"About a half hour ago. I was starting to melt. What's it like out there?"

"Intense." He could see how disappointed she was by his answer.

"But extraordinary." He told her about the old Chinese man and the burning house with the TV antenna penciled on its paper roof. "It's probably a derivation of the Yue Lan festival. An homage paid by—" A professorial tone that he abhorred had crept into his voice. "It doesn't matter. They're either sending their dead loved ones what they cherished in life, or, more than likely, what they never quite got in this world."

"What would you send me?"

"An air conditioner that works twenty-four hours a day."

Helene laughed, then fell silent. Thomas studied her. He knew enough not to reverse the question or their whole day might fall under a pall.

"By the way," she said, polishing off her coffee, "Mr. Finster left us a note. He must have slipped it under our door after you left. Did you say anything to him about our going to the caves?"

"I don't remember, Helene. I might have."

"Well, he wants to come along. We've got to get rid of him, Thomas. Once a guy like him globs on to you, you can't shake him loose."

She reached over to the night table and handed Thomas a torn sheet of ruled paper covered with an oddly meticulous script, the loopity-loop lettering found on a Hallmark card.

Dear Helene and Tom,

Hope you enjoyed last night. Maybe we can do dinner again tonight? I know a terrific restaurant that serves some great Vanduuan specialties. Also, if it would be okay, may I catch a ride with you to Baguay tomorrow?

All best,
Adam

She took the note back and crumpled it up. "You've got to tell him no, Thomas, otherwise we'll never get rid of him. He'll ruin our vacation. He's trouble, I can just tell he's trouble. There's something off about this guy, something a little scary. He's probably a drug smuggler. What the hell is in those boxes, anyhow?"

"Helene, please, I'll talk to the man."

She tilted her head back and closed her eyes. "Sorry. My head's killing me."

"I'll be right back," Thomas said, standing up.

"Don't you want to eat your breakfast first, darling?"

"Helene, let me get this over with. Okay?"

He walked down the hall and knocked on Finster's door. When no one answered, he banged again, louder this time. "Finster?" he called over the marching music. A young Vanduuan maid trundling a linen cart down the corridor smiled shyly at him. Her teeth and gums were school-brick red. "Do you know if the gentleman's in?" Thomas asked. She grinned without a shred of comprehension, then unlocked the door, nudged it open, and waddled off.

Finster's boxes were stacked in the middle of the floor. A couple were open and tufts of newspaper, like sofa stuffing, poked out of the ripped cardboard. Thomas could see a glint of glass within. "Finster, you here?" he shouted, taking a single step inside. A dozen or so tiny vials were tucked in the box's cells. Even from where he stood, he could see the thick amber liquid that filled them. "Finster?" he called again, but now it was only a ruse to justify his presence in the room. He took a step closer and picked up a vial. In the light, the liquid was transparent. The vial had no label or markings, but it wore a gold scalloped cap. He returned it to its cell, stepped back to his original position at the edge of the room, and was about to leave when he noticed some letters on the bureau. With the unscrupulousness of an anthropologist, he began to read one, all the while keeping his ear cocked for any sounds in the hall.

Dear Mr. Finestar,

I am a young country boy who is always ignored and spat upon by girls and women. I am very sad and lonely. I having no woman in the world to love. Will you help me when you come to my kampung. I have finance, or will trade pistol. I need help and talk. I am worthy of love.

Your's faithfully,
Daniel Pulug

Thomas couldn't stop himself. He read the next one.

Dear Mr. Finster,

I am Hindu.

I have bride picked out by parents, but she is still too young for marriage yet. I am a fully formed man. What to do? Mr. Sundram suggest I contact you. I am sex lover.

Yours faithfully,
Mr. Chatterjee

He knew he should leave, but he read on.

Dear Sir,

I am a man full of sex and enterprise. If your product works I will like to buy to sell here in my kampung back in jungle which has no roads, only paths. If it works, I will buy more, so if you are still selling please could you send me further information at my cousin PO Box in Vanduu. (Over)

Thomas turned the letter over.

** For any interested person.*

Ref. Selling Vanduuan drug (Mariwana)

I am also drug dealer here in my kampung and I'm interested to trade with people overseas.

Could you assist me to contact with interested people.
There five groups to chose from.

1. *attrack to dance to the beat (music)*
2. *laugh and feel funny*
3. *move about without fear*
4. *feel sleepy*
5. *to eat much*

I'm also interest to trade 20 k.g free for a gun, if interested reply soon. Please reply soon.

Yours faithfully,
Johnny Engagai

Next to the letters was Finster's replies, penned in his odd, curlicue scrawl.

Dear Mr. Pulug,
Love is not as elusive as you fear. Hope is coming—

Suddenly Thomas heard someone approaching. He stepped back into the hall and quickly shut the door. It was the young maid, hauling a stack of towels.

When she smiled at him, he felt ridiculously compelled to explain what he had been doing in Finster's room.

"I was just writing the gentleman a note," he said. She nodded enthusiastically. Obviously, she spoke no English and couldn't tell one Occidental from another.

Thomas lit a cigarette, inhaled deeply, and walked back to their room.

"Did you talk to him?" Helene asked, sitting up in bed, spine arched, shoulders contorted, nails bared, feverishly trying to get at a mosquito bite in the middle of her back. "Did you tell him we can't give him a ride to Baguay?"

"Unfortunately, he wasn't in."

"Great, now we're stuck with him."

"Helene, we're not stuck with anyone." He stretched out on the bed beside her and scratched the length of her spine.

"A little to the left . . . no, up . . . no, down."

He patiently followed the intricacies of her directions.

"Listen," he said, "I don't know if Finster's a drug smuggler or not, but I think he's . . . well, it's hard to explain exactly." He told her about the maid and the lock and the vials and the letters. "He's either a drug dealer, Helene, or he's Vanduu's equivalent of Miss Lonely-hearts."

"I don't care if he's Ann Landers in drag. We just have to get rid of him."

They napped. They could barely get themselves to leave their room, the hotel, the air-conditioning really. In the early afternoon, they made a short foray around the hotel district, poking into narrow, dusty tourist shops where the owners, reeking of hair tonic, tried to sell them everything from carved coconut soup bowls to plastic shrunken-head flashlights attached to key chains. They ate lunch and dinner at the hotel's restaurant, two of six diners amid yards and yards of white tablecloth. Thomas ordered the fruit bat stew, while Helene played it safe with the chicken à la king. In the end, they could not tell their dishes apart.

When they got back to their room, they found another note from Finster shoved under the door.

We must have just missed each other for dinner. Sorry about the screw-up. I'll swing by your room early manana to talk about our plans for Baguay.

Adam

"That's it," Helene said, balling up the note. "We've got to get rid of him now, Thomas. Please talk to him."

Thomas headed down the hall and knocked on Finster's door. He heard a thump, scrape, and the shuffle of rubber flip-flops across the floor. The door creaked open, and Finster, clad only in thongs and boxer shorts, blinked at him. His eyelids were cherry red and his voluminous blond hair, unshackled from its rubber band, spiked out in all directions.

"Didn't wake you, did I?" Thomas asked.

Finster craned his neck out into the hall. "Did they stop playing the marching music?"

"About an hour ago."

"I can handle the Muzak, but those marches fry me."

"They're not exactly sleep-inducing lullabies," Thomas said. He noticed that Finster was holding a pen. "I can come back later if you're busy."

Finster looked down and examined the pen as if he'd never seen it before. "Busy?" he said, swinging open the door. "Hardly."

The room was dark, except for the bureau lamp. In its forty-watt puddle, Thomas could just make out the pile of boxes, the letters, and Finster's writing tablet. For a moment, it looked as if Finster had been scribbling crazily, obsessively all over the top page. Then Thomas saw the lines of ink move and realized that they were ants.

"Whiskey?" Finster asked, sitting down on the edge of the bed.

"No, thanks, Adam. I really can't stay. I just dropped by to tell you that Helene and I can't take you to Baguay tomorrow. We've decided to stay in the capital for—"

"Toke?" Finster asked. He was already lighting up a joint. "I'm not exactly the hostess with the mostest, Tom. It's either whiskey or pot or—" He suddenly reeled around and opened his nightstand drawer. "Or a Hershey bar with almonds. Chocolate's a rare delicacy around here. I could make a fortune if I could get a Godiva franchise."

Thomas looked quizzically at Finster. "What the hell are you doing here, Adam?"

"I'm getting stoned, Tom."

"I meant in Vanduu, Finster."

"Import-export, as I told your lovely wife." He held out the joint. "Try it, Tom, it's the only thing I know that puts Vanduu in its correct perspective."

Thomas scrutinized the boy, then gingerly took a puff, holding fast the sweet, scalding smoke till his lungs ached. When he exhaled, he watched the smoke fly out of his mouth.

"Knock-'em-dead stuff, isn't it, Tom?"

"It's certainly powerful," Thomas said. He sat down on the edge of the bed and closed his eyes for a moment. He wanted to leave but his limbs felt as heavy as sandbags.

"One more hit?"

Thomas laughed, then shook his head no. "I've had quite enough."

Finster took another drag, then blew out a half dozen smoke rings. They drifted across the air like tiny blue hulahoops. "So what brings *you* to Vanduu, Tom?"

"Holiday, Adam."

"Our beautiful palm-fringed beaches?"

"Something like that."

"Was she a student of yours?"

"Excuse me?"

"Helene. Your wife."

"How the hell did you know I taught?"

"Don't get paranoid, Tom. You wrote down 'professor' when we registered. So was she?"

Through a woolly, dilating daze, Thomas studied the kid—the red lids, the sun-bleached curls, the packed shoulders, the loose boxer shorts covered with tiny bulldogs. "Matter of fact, she was," he lied.

"So, how old was she when you met? Eighteen? Twenty?"

"Does it really matter, Finster?"

"Just curious. Freshman? Sophomore?"

"It's none of your goddamn business."

"Hey, you're not exactly the typical all-American couple, Tom. I'm just making conversation."

"Really?" Thomas said. He'd seen Finster scrutinizing his wife. He understood exactly what the kid was up to, and chitchat played no part of it. More than anyone, he knew what the off-kilter beauty of a woman like Helene could evoke, especially to a boy in the middle of nowhere. He, himself, had spent his twenty-eighth birthday jacking off in a mud-and-wattle hut to the image of Brett McGrath, the big-breasted, quinine-tinged wife of his mentor and best friend in the Amazon. Normally he'd have sloughed off the kid's rudeness, but tonight he wanted to belt him for his unflagging, zonked-out, unstoppable youth. He wasn't even dead yet, and the Finsters of the world were already moving in on Helene.

He grasped the edge of the mattress and stood up, figuring he'd better leave before he took a swing at Oceania's Miss Lonelyhearts, or whoever the hell he was. "Sleep well, Adam," he said.

"You're leaving?"

"Helene's waiting for me." In bed, he was tempted to add.

"Give her my best."

Fat chance, Thomas thought.

"Am I going to see you guys again?"

"It's a small island, Finster."

He opened the door and slammed it behind him. The hall undulated, and he crossed it as one crosses a flimsy footbridge. When he got back to their room, Helene was asleep, curled on her side, naked. The sight of her cut through his heart. He got undressed and slid in beside her. The shelf of her hip was a hallucinatory white. Her hands were tucked between her thighs. Her breasts rose and fell as she breathed. He pressed himself against her, hoping beyond hope that her beauty would take over, that its sheer undeniability would jar something. He'd even settle for his jealousy of Finster to do the trick. He could feel the give of her thighs, smell the pungency of her skin. He closed his eyes and tried to rally desire, but no matter how hard he concentrated, he could not move yearning out of his mind and into his body. He grazed his lips along her shoulder. By her steady breathing, he knew he hadn't woke her, and he was grateful. Whenever he tried to touch her these days, he could feel degrees of sadness, as one feels degrees of temperature, emanating from her skin. He pressed his mouth against her neck. He felt weirdly hollow, as if the conflagration that had once made up his being had been burned out of him. He rubbed his soft penis against her. It wasn't exactly numbness he felt, it was more like nonexistence.

After a while, she stirred and rolled over. He slowly stroked the length and breadth of her back, easing her into deep sleep again.

Then, with phantasmagorical clarity on the back of his closed lids, he envisioned himself entering her. Lack of desire wasn't the problem, it was the memory of desire that was killing him.

The Vanduuans have a way of seeing without focusing their gaze, and Finster almost had it perfected. The head tilts. The eyelids twitch. In a calculated daze, the pupils float toward a noise, then glide on.

Someone's boots were clambering over the bus's roof. No one appeared to look up except Finster and the Vanduuan kid across the aisle, who was high on solvents. Finster disapproved of solvents. He considered himself a connoisseur of altered states, and solvents were, to say the least, the McHigh of highs. He, himself, had brought two bud-filled joints for the four-hour trip to Baguay, but now, between the roadblock and spontaneous looting and his countless trips to the bus's loo for a puff, he found himself still less than two miles from the center of the city and down to a single roach. The bus hadn't budged in an hour.

Outside, he could see blurred shapes hurtling by—a lobbed bottle, an army jeep, the white sneakers of a bounding looter. The bus's windows were so darkly tinted that Finster could barely make out what was going on, but that was okay with him. It was the third riot he'd been caught in in less than two months. The first had been sparked by the rape and murder of a Vanduuan bar girl by an Australian tourist: The man had been sent home due to "lack of evidence." The second fracas had flared up over the blinding of a Vanduuan maid by her Minaphoran employer: The employer had sprayed insecticide in the maid's eyes during a dispute over pay. Today's rampage had begun with rumors that Amalgamated International Enterprises, the American company that had built Vanduu's power plant, was purposefully turning the juice off every other night to remind the Vanduuans who was in charge. The rioting never got beyond the cardboard shantytowns that ringed the capital. The security police moved in to form a human barricade between the looters and the shops, the slums and the tourist sights.

The police were privately financed by foreign investors, American and Minaphoran mostly, and made up of ex–Marcos's boys, Indonesian mercenaries, and a smattering of Vanduuans, country yokels from the outer islands who joined up for the quick bucks, spiffy uniforms, and heady power.

Finster stayed neutral. After all, yokels with money were his best customers. He had his boxes with him, strapped with bungee cords into the adjacent seats. Not trusting the bus's roof racks, he'd actually purchased first-class tickets for his vials, and now he felt justified. Another set of boots were clopping overhead.

Next to the rheumy-eyed driver, who, in Finster's opinion, also looked stoned, hung a small transistor radio. It was squawking out American disco tunes from the seventies. Between "Shake Your Booty" and "Hot Stuff," the deejay quipped, "You chew the betel nut, we'll spin the hits."

The marijuana was beginning to wear off and Finster felt a humongous headache coming on. He cracked open the window to see if the frigging bus would ever get moving. A knot of masked boys were running down the street, hauling a bucket of red paint. Whenever they came to a sign with foreign words on it—Colonel Sanders, Kee Wah Yen Mufflers—they blotted it out and painted Vanduuan over it. The script looked like crescents and halves of moons. At a Hindi movie billboard, they splashed out everything but the leading lady—a comely, slightly mustachioed girl in a negligee. Her heavy breasts defied gravity.

Finster closed the window and sank back against the creaky upholstery. Between the pot and the zeppelin-size bosoms and Donna Summer's orgasmic cries, he dreamt of Helene—actually, for the past thirty-six hours, he'd thought of little else. There was something about her—a steely vulnerability, a negligent beauty—that knocked him breathless. He knew she'd been on the brink of tears in the bar, and he was curious—*no,* crazed to know why. He figured it had something to do with the old man, but Helene hadn't given a clue. The woman had class, not like his usual fare of karaoke girls and strippers. They were sweet kids, but they giggled nonstop, and flattered him ridiculously, and wept when he wouldn't marry them, and tasted of foreign spices that left him sick with loneliness. When he'd kissed Helene, when he'd held her in his arms, he'd felt like he was holding something as rare and fragile and hard as Steuben glass.

He shut his eyes and pictured himself standing outside her window two nights ago. He could see her spectacular breasts in the moonlight. He envisioned himself entering the room, brushing back the netting, and crawling into bed beside her. He saw his hand, with its bitten nails, caress her nipple, cup the whole splendid globe in his palm and kiss it.

A megaphone suddenly blasted him out of his reverie. An army jeep screeched by and the rioters scattered. The bus finally shuddered into motion. It rolled past the makeshift roadblock of burning tires, hoops of fire. The smoke and stench were ghastly, even with the window shut. Through the tinted glass, the slums seemed shrouded in perpetual dusk. Only the sun hinted at noon. It burned vaguely over the tar-paper roofs, like an eclipse.

Once the bus cleared the melee, the driver, stoned and fearless, floored the accelerator, lurching the bus into a jerky zoom. Vanduu ticked by in a frenetic wind. At the top of the mountain, Finster cracked open his window again to catch one last glimpse of the city. In all that urban sprawl, the shantytown riot looked insignificant, save for the fact that it had thrown the capital, a gummy puddle of smog really, into massive gridlock.

"I don't think we've budged in twenty minutes," Helene said. "Maybe we should just get out and walk. Could you ask the driver where the fuck we are?"

Thomas leaned forward and rested his hand on the trishaw driver's shoulder. The man was his age, or at least looked as old as him. Thomas loathed the idea of being pedaled around by someone who was probably more exhausted than he was. On the advice of the toothless bellhop, they'd left their car in front of the hotel and hired the driver to take them to see the temples.

"Where are we?" Thomas shouted over the rumble and sputter of clogged traffic. "Is this congestion normal?"

"Yes, no problem, you be at Snake temple very, very soon," the driver answered politely.

"Christ, let me see the map," Helene said.

While she pored over the map, Thomas looked up and down the street, or what he could see of it behind the throbbing buses and the revving pedicabs. Between the sun and the fumes, he felt truly ill. Now and again, a souped-up World War II jeep crammed with soldiers in snappy new uniforms honked and bullied its way through the congestion. Some of the soldiers wore Ray•Bans and carried what looked like tommy guns from a black and white James Cagney movie. Thomas had the unsettling feeling that the soldiers' presence wasn't exactly copacetic, even for Vanduu.

He sank back against the brittle seat and turned to Helene.

She was still bent over the map, oblivious of all else. "We're here and the temple is there," she said, pointing to a mishmash of lines that, in the blistering light, made no sense to him. "It's walkable."

Thomas gave the driver a crisp American ten, then stepped out of the trishaw into the snarl of bumpers. Helene and he zigzagged their way to the curb and headed down a side street, out of the thick exhaust, through wafts of sweet incense, then back into a zone of ghastly fumes.

For a moment, Thomas experienced one of his global shifts; one sandaled foot was still in Vanduu, but the other had transcended hemispheres and touched down on a garbage-strewn street in Sâo Paulo. He leaned against a money changer's shack and took a deep breath. His vision jerked back into focus, but sweat dripped into his right eye.

"If you're not feeling well, Thomas, let's go back to the hotel, for Christ's sake."

"I'm perfectly all right," he lied, and started to cross the street, six more lanes of head-to-toe traffic, but stumbled over an old woman's outstretched leg. She sat on the sidewalk, under a red beach umbrella, hawking Cup-O-Noodles heated on a Sterno flame. There was no can of Sterno. The little flame burned directly on the concrete, as if a hole had been jabbed through the crust of the earth and its fire poked up here.

Stooping over, Thomas tried to apologize, but the old hawker ignored him. She cupped her hands around her feeble fire. A new glut of sweat rolled into his eyes, and for a moment the wobbly flame appeared to proliferate until the old woman's hands, the umbrella, the sidewalk, the traffic were all brilliance and instability.

"I must sit down," he said, sinking down beside the old woman. If it wasn't for the look of unadulterated terror on Helene's face, he might have been content to rest in the shade of the umbrella all afternoon.

"What's wrong? Oh my God, Thomas, what's wrong?"

He shrugged to indicate all was well.

"Are you all right? Can you get up?"

"Of course," he said, without conviction.

"I'm going to find a doctor."

Unable to reach her hand, he gripped her ankle, stunned by how fragile the bone felt. He wouldn't let go.

"Helene, I'm fine. Really. It's just the heat."

"You're sitting on a fucking sidewalk. You're not fine."

"Everyone else is sitting, too."

All up and down the street, fixed as boulders, men and women sat on filthy blankets, or scraps of cardboard, or specks of shade, trying to peddle the chintz and bangles of the far-flung world. Thomas and Helene were the only tourists in sight.

"I'm going to get you a cold drink," she said.

He was about to stop her, but changed his mind and nodded gratefully. While Helene was gone, he leaned forward and rested his sunburnt brow on his pink knees, to the discomfort and irritation of the old woman beside him.

Helene returned with a sweating bottle of premixed Kool-Aid. The liquid inside was the color of key lime pie. She squatted down beside him and held the cold bottle against his brow. "Does that help?" she asked. "Everything else was unrefrigerated and boiling. This is the only stuff I could find that was cold, safety sealed, and—well, American."

She opened the bottle, then handed it to Thomas.

"Wasn't this the flavor they served in Jonestown?" he asked.

"I believe it was," she said, smiling. But he could see how strained the smile was.

He took a couple of long swigs, then gave the bottle back. She merely wet her lips with the remaining sugar water. "Do you want to sit for a while, Thomas?"

He wanted to sit there all day, but he could sense her fear sharpening with every second that passed.

"I'll get up," he said. "Are we far from the hotel?"

"With all the traffic, I don't think we got more than a few blocks."

He braced himself and slowly rose to his feet. He could barely feel his legs: They were numb and queerly light, as if they were made of Styrofoam. But he would not let Helene help him.

"What was I thinking? What in the name of Jesus fucking shit-ball Christ could I have been thinking?" Helene said as soon as they walked into their sweltering, pink room. Thomas went over to the bed and stretched out, while she strode up to the air conditioner and jabbed at the buttons. When it wouldn't start, she actually punched the contraption to life. "The world is filled with little paradises but I managed to find hell. I could have chosen Tahiti. I could have picked the Marquesas. But no, I had to drag you to this filthy little incinerator in the middle of nowhere."

He closed his eyes. He was too spent to argue.

"How you doing? You okay?" she asked gently.

He nodded.

She went into the bathroom and came back with a wet face cloth. Perching on the edge of their bed, she wiped his face and throat, then wrung the rag out over the frayed carpet and laid it across his forehead. He caught her wrist and kissed her palm. He could feel the mattress start to quake as she began frenetically tapping her foot. "I'm so sorry, Thomas. Let's just go home. I hate this place."

Even with his eyes shut, he knew she was crying. He kept his lips pressed against her palm, feeling the arduous responsibility to infuse this moment, like so many others of late, with false hope, feigned levity, whatever it took to keep her from sinking. He couldn't allow her to go home in defeat; he knew exactly what awaited them if she did—a sadness that would eat away at them faster than any cancer. As long as they kept moving, she could keep her illusion that their marriage might return to normalcy, that he might become his old self, and that if they remained in perpetual motion, they might somehow elude fate.

"Sweetheart, we've only been here three days. It took us longer to fly here."

"I don't care," she said.

"Let's go to the Vatu caves tomorrow. We were planning to go there anyhow. They're supposed to be spectacular. Didn't Mr. Khan say the caves were the eighth wonder of the world?" He smiled with forced enthusiasm and lifted the rag. "Besides, it's always a lot cooler in the mountains."

"How do you know?"

"It always is, Helene. You know that as well as I do."

"But this island is a living hell on earth. The mountains are probably bubbling volcanoes, the caves are probably spewing fire."

"They're not bubbling volcanoes, Helene."

Forcing himself to sit up, he swung his feet over the side of the bed. His legs now felt as heavy as I beams. "There's something about the climate in the brochure Mr. Khan gave us." He rifled through their suitcase and found Mr. Khan's ten-page, handwritten, mimeographed brochure entitled *You're in Paradise with Paradise Tours!* When he started skimming the text, he realized that what had initially charmed him back in New York, now struck him as abysmally depressing.

> *Please look up "Paradise" in your dictionary and you will find as one of its definitions, Vanduu. A small, splendific—just mix splendid and terrific—island south of the Philippines and north of New Guinea, with palm-fringed beaches and a boogie-on-down capital with sumptuous restaurants and swinging nightclubs. Get those disco shoes out!*

Thomas ran his finger a little further down the page.

> *In our temperate mountains around the lovely colonial city of Baguay are the world-famous Vatu caves . . .*

"It says it's ten to twenty degrees cooler in the mountains," he lied.

She lay her head on his lap. "Do you really think it'll be better there?"

He leaned back and closed his eyes again. "Helene, I'm sure of it."

They left early the next morning. Helene drove so that Thomas could rest. As soon as they passed the shantytowns, and the knots of visored soldiers, and the gummy black remnants of what looked, to Thomas at least, like burnt tires, the landscape turned mountainous, then cracked open into deep gorges. The cliffs were rust red. Jungle tumbled out of every crevasse, sprouted from every crack—monster ferns, ladder vines, moss as green as AstroTurf. Now and again, a waterfall fell in a mile-long streak, making its own clouds. The clouds ascended the red cliffs in slow motion. Where the gorges widened into valleys, rice paddies tiered the slopes. The world reflected in their watery squares was pink, gold, and silver. The irrigation systems—drips, canals, spinning buckets, bamboo waterwheels—looked like Rube Goldberg contraptions. Some of the villages stood on stilts, while others formed miniature tin towns crammed on mud islands. Here and there, an abandoned car was left to rot by the side of the road, but even these looked resplendent. Jungle had transformed them. Thomas and Helene passed what looked like a topiary sedan, a topiary Mack truck cab, an overturned lichen chassis.

Where nature and culture collide had been the focus of Thomas's research, or, at least, what he had written about in his first seminal book, *The Origin of Trash.* The book proposed the theory that what truly separates "primitive" societies from "civilized" ones is the manufacture of refuse; that primitive societies work like perpetual-motion machines, not taking in more than they can absorb by utilizing the flux and energy of nature, whereas linear societies work like engines, consuming raw material and giving off waste. It wasn't the originality of his premise that had catapulted him to renown—after all, many anthropologists were dabbling in similar ideas—it was his love of language and nature that had infused a six-hundred-page chronicle on the history of garbage with compelling lyricism. He did countless field studies after that, and wrote seven more books, but nothing came close to his first.

He cranked his seat back a smidgen, just enough to rest but not fall asleep, and watched with odd detachment the rush of greenery, the variegated paddies, the waterfalls ending in pools of quicksilver. It was the detachment one feels toward an ex-lover whose beauty no longer causes jealousy or rancor, just numbing nothingness. In truth, he felt so tired, he'd really rather close his eyes and sleep.

But he knew Helene was watching him, so he forced himself to stay awake. To please her, to allow her to believe that their coming to Vanduu had been worth it, he acted deeply moved by all he saw. Amid this landscape of vast beauty, he pretended to love the thing he once genuinely loved in order to make his young wife happy.

Without taking her eyes off the road, without even looking at him, Helene knew exactly what Thomas was doing, and felt even sadder.

All the hotels in Baguay were booked, or, at least, the three they found. One concierge, a barefoot teenage boy who tended the front desk, told them about an SDA missionary who took in guests, but when they drove past the missionary's tin church, the door was chained shut and the windows boarded over. A fruit vendor mentioned a row of Chinese guest houses on the far side of town, but his directions were so vague, they immediately got lost. Night was dropping fast. With mounting panic, Helene cruised the main drag, a hodgepodge of crumbling European facades, squat churches, and one gold-domed mosque, looking for a boardinghouse, but nothing they saw hinted of rest. Finally, she insisted that they return to the first hotel, where she planned to get down on her hands and knees and beg the clerk to let them sleep on a sofa in the air-conditioned lobby. After yesterday's debacle, she didn't want Thomas sleeping in the car. She made a U-turn and was heading back up the road when, in the periphery of her vision, she thought she spied Finster's blond ponytail floating above a crowd of Vanduuans.

She jabbed at the brakes. "Did you see who I saw?" she asked. When Thomas shrugged, she pointed out Finster in the fast-fading light. "Should we ask him where there's a hotel, Thomas?"

"We'll be stuck with him, Helene."

She didn't care. She knew Finster would know where there was a decent hotel and a restaurant that wouldn't poison them. She also knew that if Thomas should feel faint again, he'd know where to find a doctor. "For God's sake, Thomas, I have to pee. I've had to pee since three o'clock this afternoon. I'm so hot and tired that if he knows where there's a clean hotel with an American toilet and edible food, he can move in with us."

"Oh, I don't think so," Thomas said. With halting reluctance, he cranked down his window and shouted to Finster.

Finster squinted in their direction, did a double take, grinned, then trotted over in his flopping zoris.

"I thought you guys were staying in the capital for a while." He hunched over and peered through Thomas's open window at Helene. "Hi," he said softly.

"The capital got a little hot and hectic," Thomas said.

"They're still looting?"

"Who's looting?"

To avoid Finster's probing gaze, Helene rolled down her window and stuck her head out. "It's like an oven. It's like putting your head into a goddamn oven. The brochure said it would be cooler up here."

"Really?" Finster smiled, leaning his chapped elbows on Thomas's window gutter. "I thought hot air rises."

"We need a hotel, Adam. Got any bright ideas?" Thomas asked.

"Why don't you stay where I'm staying? Best digs in town."

"Where's that?"

"The Vatu Chalets."

"We tried it. They're full up."

"You joking? The place is so empty, it's haunted. The kid at the front desk is just too lazy to open up another chalet. I'll talk to the owner, Farouk. He's a friend of mine."

"Would you, Adam?" Helene said.

"It would be my pleasure." He reached for the back-door handle. "May I?"

"Get in, Finster," Thomas said.

Finster slid in, then leaned forward and rested his chin on the front seat between them.

The Vatu Chalets were a half dozen plywood cabins scattered along a path through the jungle. As soon as they swung into the parking lot and Helene killed the engine, Finster tried to catch her eye. He thought if he could just get her to look at him, he'd be able to glean whether or not their kiss had the same lingering effect on her as it had on him, but Helene seemed to be looking at everything in the known universe except Finster—the A-frame stilt lobby, the swarms of gnats, the pregnant goat eating a Pringles box out of a garbage can, Thomas's hawklike profile in the last spokes of daylight. It hardly mattered; just being in her presence filled him with a heady surge of hope.

They started up the steep steps to the lobby. Finster noticed that Helene firmly took hold of Thomas's elbow. The gesture was protective, almost nurselike, and he could see it bothered Thomas. He was a step or two below them. From this angle, he could just make out a hint of Helene's upper thighs under the fringe of her cutoffs, and they were perfect. Once again, he couldn't imagine what she was doing with this old man.

When they opened the lobby doors, the teenage concierge was squatting on the floor, preparing a wad of betel. He managed to pop it into his mouth before Finster ordered him to the front desk and began berating him for not renting his friends a chalet. Actually, Finster liked the boy (they'd shared a joint earlier that afternoon), but he wanted to impress Helene with his worldly authority, his American can-do.

After the concierge sullenly shuffled off to find some fresh linen, Finster suggested that Helene and Thomas go to their chalet, relax, and take a shower. He said he'd be back in an hour with a feast for all three of them. They didn't argue. They looked grateful. They were standing under the lobby's listless ceiling fan, and though Finster couldn't quite put his finger on it, there was something sad about them.

He trotted off to Auntie Eknilang's, the local cook, to rally her into preparing something other than her usual fare, Spam sushi. Matter of fact, he emphatically told the old woman that tinned *anything*—be it corn beef or whole chicken—was not to appear on the menu. He wanted something special, something native—steamed land crabs and taro cakes, or a grilled barracuda and sago. He'd even settle for stewed fruit bat if it was prepared with yams. He slipped the old woman an extra ten, then jogged back to the hotel to prepare the dining gazebo, a screened octagonal shack next to the swimming pool. He even hired the concierge's sisters, two bull-necked girls, to haul out and wash some real china dishes.

Then he took a shower, cinched back his hair, combed his mustache, and slipped into a fresh pair of Hawaiian trunks. Since there would be no alcohol served tonight (the Chalets' owner was Muslim), he took two, three eye-watering hits off a joint to level his nerves.

Around eight, he swung by Helene and Thomas's cabin. They were fully dressed, supine on the bed: Thomas was asleep, Helene was staring at the ceiling, and once again, Finster had the ill-defined sense that something was amiss in their relationship. Though Helene gently stirred Thomas awake, Finster intuited a frayed tension under her seemingly attentive veneer.

He loped beside her all the way to the gazebo.

"Quite a feast," Thomas said, peeling open the screen door.

In the center of the gazebo sat a low round table laden with food—slabs of fried Spam, corn beef hash, a plate of taro mash the consistency of rabbit glue, and a big bowl of Top Ramen noodles.

"I told the woman not to serve Spam," Finster said. "I told her not to serve tinned *anything*."

"It's fine, Finster, really," Thomas said. "It looks delicious." He sat down on a throw of pillows, Helene sat down next to him, and Finster wedged himself in beside her.

"I'd stick with the noodle soup," Finster told Helene. He ladled out a bowl for her, carefully skimming off the amoeba-shaped globules of fat. Then he fixed one for Thomas and himself as well. "So, did you guys come to see the caves or the psychosurgeries?"

"The caves," Helene said.

Finster smiled. "They're awesome. They look like . . ." He could barely remember what they looked like: He hadn't been there in years. "They look like . . . like a movie set, only they're real." He couldn't believe how idiotic he sounded, more like the San Fernando Valley boy he once was than the Gauguin figure he hoped Helene perceived him to be: He knew he should stop smoking so much pot. "I'd love to show them to you," he said. "Unfortunately, I have some business to attend to tomorrow, but I could take you there on Sunday."

"Thanks, Finster, but I'm sure we can manage," Thomas said.

"Hey, Tom, trust me, you need a guide. You can't just wander around the caves by yourselves. They're filled with live shells. The caves were an ammo dump during the war. At least once every couple of years some Japanese honeymooners go up in a puff."

"Must put a damper on tourism."

"Actually, it gives the caves a romantic charge."

Thomas put down his soup. He'd barely touched it. "Do they still perform psychosurgeries?"

"To be honest, I've never seen one. But my customers swear by them."

"Customers for what?" Helene asked.

"For this." Finster dug into the pocket of his aloha shirt and pulled out a vial. He set it down gingerly on Helene's plate, as one might serve a dessert truffle. "Smell it."

"Am I going to get high or something?"

"Just smell it."

Helene glanced at Thomas, then uncapped the vial and waved it under her nose. "Oh my God, it's like . . . like essence of Woolworth." She closed her eyes and sniffed again. "I'm having a Proustian experience. I'm back in aisle six, between the Whitman samplers and the hair spray, and my whole childhood is unfolding before me. How did you bottle this? *Why* did you bottle it?"

"It's perfume," he said defensively. "With pheromones. It's a sexual attractant, like an aphrodisiac. I didn't come up with the scent, I just import the stuff. Among other things," he added.

"It has human pheromones in it?" Thomas asked.

"Actually, they're pig pheromones, but hey, it's a pig culture."

"And the locals believe it works?"

"Big time. And *they* really like the scent. *They* think of it as some kind of American love potion," he said, staring at Helene. But she wasn't listening. She seemed to have abruptly lost interest in the whole conversation, and he wondered why.

"How do they even know about it?" Thomas asked.

"I advertise in the local rags, and in *Guns and Ammo. Guns and Ammo* has a whopping circulation in these islands." He turned to Helene. "You can come with me tomorrow on my delivery rounds if you want. My customers are pretty interesting, and to say the least, it's off the beaten track."

Thomas shook his head and smiled. "So you're an entrepreneurial Malinowski of a sort."

"Malino-who?"

"Bronislaw Malinowski. He was an anthropologist who wrote a book about Melanesia called *The Sexual Life of Savages.*"

"Like the title," Finster said, grinning. He helped himself to one of Thomas's cigarettes, lit it, then tried to catch Helene's eye again, but it was hopeless. "Actually, I see myself more in Conradian terms. A Kurtz without the horror, the horror hypocrisy."

Back in their room, Thomas said, "Can you believe this guy? He sees himself as a workaday Kurtz? I wonder if he means Conrad's Kurtz, or Coppola's Marlon Brando?" He peeled off his T-shirt, then wiped his face with it. "Should we take him up on his offer? Just the idea of seeing this zonked-out kid trying to pass himself off as a shaman should be worth the price of admission. It's an amazing concept, Helene. Finster has managed to turn himself into the quintessential antithesis of everything I've ever believed in. He's not only interfering with the local culture, he's selling the Vanduuans their own religion in a bottle, one that smells like Woolworth. I can't imagine what the Vanduuans think of him. Do you think they think he has magic?"

"I don't particularly feel like driving through remote villages, where the men are so desperate for sex they're willing to try his lunatic perfume, in order to find out." She walked over to the window and picked at the wooden sash. "But you go if you want."

She hated the tone of her voice—a clenched whine counterpointed with rumbling ire. She could see how intrigued Thomas was by Finster's business. It was the first time he'd been intrigued by anything even remotely resembling his work in almost a year.

"You're right, it's probably ridiculous to go."

She didn't answer him. She pulled off a splinter and continued picking at the sash. The last thing she wanted was for them to spend the day with Finster driving around the countryside peddling sex in a bottle. The very idea of it seemed so ironically sad to her, she doubted she could bear it, and she was furious with Thomas for not understanding that.

"Forget it, Helene, we'll stay here. Or we'll go to the caves by ourselves."

"For Christ's sake, if you want to go, just go, Thomas."

He sat down on the bed, put his elbows on his knees, his head in his hands. When he finally looked up, his face was the color of ashen wax. "What do you want from me, Helene? I thought you wanted me to take an interest in work. I thought we were supposed to do this together." He pressed the heels of his hands against his eyes. "Tell me what you want from me."

She could hardly tell him that she wanted to go home *tonight,* that Finster's persistent, pining stare only exasperated her loss, that she couldn't handle his being ill any longer, that she had to know what was going to happen to him, that not knowing was killing her as virulently as anything inside him, and that if she lost him, she couldn't imagine what she'd do.

Instead, in a voice so saccharine that it made her teeth ache, she said, "Just make sure that you don't exert yourself, darling."

"For God's sake, Helene, stop treating me like a fucking invalid!"

Thomas walked into the bathroom, slammed the door behind him, and set off a deluge in the shower. Helene stood outside the door, tempted to apologize, but she knew if she did, Thomas would want to talk, and if they talked, it would be about his illness, and she couldn't bear to discuss it: She still held fast to the slim hope that if they didn't discuss it, it might not be real.

She shed her tank top and cutoffs, slipped into her bathing suit and robe, then shouted that she was going for a swim, grabbed a pack of Thomas's cigarettes, and headed to the pool. The stone path was strung with Japanese lanterns, most of which were blown out. The jungle was flush against the path, a humming, whooshing mass of abrupt blackness. She hurried from one tiny island of luminosity to another. At the pool, she shrugged off the robe and dove in. The water was as warm as human blood. Coming up for a breath, she had the unnerving sense that something or someone was watching her, but she told herself that she always felt like prey beside the jungle. She swam over to the shallow end and stood up. Out of a corner of her eye, she caught the flare of a Zippo, smelled a whiff of marijuana, and knew that Finster was out there. She turned and stared into the blackness where the flash had just been to let him know that she knew he was watching her. Then she held the stare an extra tick to make sure he knew not to come near. She hauled herself out of the pool and lay supine on the cement, looking up at the slew of stars. One by one, she smoked Thomas's cigarettes down to stubs, all the while knowing that Finster was studying her. As ashamed as she was, she needed him to study her, appraise her, because in truth, being desired was the only thing she had right now to keep the unknown at bay.

Thomas had no desire to spend the day with Finster tooling around the countryside peddling the kid's perfumes. His enthusiasm for Finster's business had been solely for Helene's benefit, to make her think that work, even in the guise of studying Finster's dime-store shamanism, could still intrigue him, but now that she wasn't coming, the ruse seemed pointless. Worse than pointless. Enervating.

He sat in the idling car, smoking his fourth cigarette of the morning, waiting for Finster to show up with his boxes. When the kid finally appeared, scuffing across the crushed coral parking lot, and saw that Helene wasn't joining them, his cocky grin became a frozen little shadow of itself. This gave Thomas great pleasure.

He unlocked Finster's door and revved the engine.

"Where to? It's your show, Adam."

Finster slid in beside him, set down his boxes, glumly pointed north, and they rolled off.

For the first hour or so, they drove past palm-thatched kampungs where rag-clad villagers stared out at them from stippled shadows. Mostly, the job entailed stopping at shacks, delivering perfume, like you deliver milk. Sometimes a desperate villager would run up to the car and, in a singsong whine, beg Finster to give him a vial on credit, but mostly, the men and boys obediently poured their tin coins into Finster's open palms. Each sale was accompanied by a round of crude jokes, or double entendres, or licentious winks. Now and again, a man would ask for Finster's advice on how to be loved, or please a woman, or, for that matter, *just find a woman.* One man confessed that after his wife's tenth child, her *wila* was too big for him to fill, that copulating with her was like copulating with the sea. Another man complained of too many erections and too few girls. One elderly farmer, who'd just purchased his second wife, a child bride, lived in terror of not being able to satisfy her.

By early afternoon, Thomas didn't think he could bear to hear another crude joke or heartrending tale. He didn't think he could tolerate the company of men and boys for whom the world consisted of sexual yearning—or nothing. There were only a couple of vials left in Finster's boxes. When they finally pulled up to what Thomas prayed was the last shack, he told Finster he'd prefer to wait in the car.

"Your call, Tom," Finster said, stepping out onto the dirt road. "Back in five."

Thomas watched Finster as he bounded up the shack's steps to tap on the splintery jamb beside the hanging tarp door. Two boys and an elderly man came out and pumped Finster's hand. The old man was bent at a forty-five-degree angle, as if he'd been struck by a falling boulder or tree or meteor but had somehow managed to survive. The two boys leaned against the shack's flimsy wall, but the old man squatted down, all hump and elbows and knees, like an insect.

Thomas put his elbow on the window gutter and rested his cheek on the crook of his arm.

Even in the shade of the tree, the sun blustered through, scattering white hot glyphs across the dash. The mosquitoes were intolerable. Their incessant hum was like the drone of heat itself.

He rolled up the window, but the sound continued. It grew incrementally louder until Thomas realized it had nothing to do with the mosquitoes. It was inside his head, within his ear, whirling down the dark canals toward chaos, and he thought, This is what one hears before one blacks out. But he felt weirdly alert, hyperconscious. The motor was running, the air conditioner was whirring, the boys were laughing loudly, but that only added to the gulf between the buzz and bustle outside, and the hollow rush within.

Then the world, all of it—the trees, the shack, the people—shrank minusculely, as if everyone and everything had agreed simultaneously to take a step backward, away from him. He shut his eyes. When he looked again, Finster and the boys had shrunk even further and now wore nimbuses of light. He knew the nimbuses were caused by the condensation of his breath on the window glass, that Finster and the boys sported his breath, and all the colors his breath gave life to, as men sport hats. They were again laughing at some bawdy joke that Finster had told, and Thomas watched them from a solitude deeper than he'd ever imagined.

When they got back, Helene was waiting on the bungalow steps. Thomas could tell by the incline of her head, the tap of her foot, the way she picked at the blistered paint on the railing, that she'd been sitting there for some time. When she spied them, she waved to Finster, then motioned Thomas inside. He plodded up the steps, closed the door behind him, and sat down on the end of their bed. She perched on his lap and cupped his face in her palms. She kissed him, then ran a fingernail along his collarbone and under his shirt. She joked about the perfume and how he must have tried it, because she was under its spell.

Thomas closed his eyes. He could sense how lonely she was. He knew she must have spent the afternoon planning this scene, rehearsing it: Her coquettishness—so out of character—had the bathos of bad acting.

He lay back on the bed and she stretched out beside him, burrowing her face against his chest. Normally, he'd stroke her cheek, caress her neck, touch the whorl of her ear, but he couldn't get himself to do it. He was still back in the car, in that droning chamber of solitude. Helene sat up, unbuttoned her shirt, then grasped his wrist and placed his hand on her breast. He cupped it, but his hand felt like someone else's. His remoteness horrified him, and he could see it devastated her.

He wanted to tell her that he hadn't come back yet, that he was trying to get back to her, but he couldn't.

"I can't," he whispered. His voice had no cadence, no warmth, and that scared him even more. When he tried to explain where he was, when he tried to tell her about the car and the hum and the desolation, his mind jammed solid, froze. The words came out encased in ice. After a while, he stopped trying.

"Don't go," he said. "Stay with me," he said.

She lay down beside him, but she lay facing the wall.

Helene lay by Thomas's side until dusk obliterated the walls, the furniture, the netting. Her left hand had long ago gone numb beneath her head; her skin was filmed with sleeper's sweat. When she finally sat up, the sheer motion cooled her down. She looked over at Thomas—mouth open, dead to the world. Only the steady hum of his breath, even as a respirator, let her know he was okay. Leaning over, she lightly touched—no, palpated his face, feeling the contour of his profile on her palm. She could almost sense their whole history from that touch—her whole history: After all, she'd been with him since she was a girl. She tilted her head back against the headboard and closed her eyes. If only he had touched her—she hadn't asked for anything else—it would have made all the difference. She brushed her hand against his cheek and the papery folds of his throat. The skin felt so dry it almost seemed friable. She got up and walked over to the window. The massive jungle was blotting out what remained of the day.

She slipped on her bathing suit, grabbed her robe and a couple of cigarettes, and headed to the pool. She dove in and made for the deepest point, the steel drain with its gummy leaves. She held her breath until the back of her eyes ached, until release and air was all she craved.

When she emerged, Finster was standing by the deep end, clad only in swimming trunks, his blond calves level with her face. He was holding a towel, not the cheesecloth-thin rags that the hotel issued, but a big fat terry-cloth spread.

"Where did you get that, Finster? Ransack a Hilton?"

'There are no Hiltons in Vanduu, Helene."

He held out the towel.

"Actually," she said, grasping the pool's mildewy, tiled edge and pulling herself out, "I prefer to drip-dry."

She stretched out on the warm cement, in her own puddled effigy, and folded her hands behind her head, all the while aware of Finster's gaze. "Could you fetch me a cigarette, Adam? They're by my robe."

"Perhaps you'd like to try one of mine," he said, plucking out a joint from the pocket of his trunks.

"I'd rather have a scotch."

"Sorry. The hotel's dry. The owner's Muslim."

"I suppose the Koran gives the green light on grass."

"Not exactly. But there's not much an infidel can do. Muhammed says, 'Just say no.'"

She laughed despite herself and took the joint. Holding it like a cigarette, she leaned into the almond-shaped flame of Finster's Zippo and took a deep drag. The smoke singed her lungs, but she held it fast. When she exhaled, she watched the smoke spiral up into the enormous night. She lay back on the cement and took another long hit. And another. She smoked it down to the stub. When she finally felt dizzy and distant and buzzed, when Finster seemed like a two-dimensional cartoon and the jungle an inky backdrop, she handed it back to him.

"Lucky I come prepared," he said, pulling out another joint.

He sat down beside her and lit up. She closed her eyes and felt the ground pitch and yield. She heard a hoot somewhere overhead but it sounded harmless. She felt the chlorinated water flash off her skin, as if someone were drying her with fire.

Suddenly she sat up. "Fuck," she said. "I'm being eaten alive." She started scratching her arms.

"Let me help," Finster said, running his hand over her shoulders. He wrapped the towel around her. "I have some calamine lotion in my room."

She thought, Neither of us are even bothering to pretend.

She stood up, grabbed her robe, and followed him to his bungalow. When he opened the door, the room looked so neat that she had an inkling he'd tidied it up for just this occasion. She sat cross-legged on the bed while he applied the cold lotion to her back. He dabbed it on as meticulously as a nurse would, and she was curious to see how he'd transform this innocent touch. After he capped the lotion, he started scratching her bites. The drag of his bitten nails across these points of fire felt exquisite. He moved his hand in concentric circles, wider and wider, each revolution veering closer to her breasts.

When she gave no hint of stopping him, he let his hand creep under her arm and into her damp bathing suit. He cupped her breast like a man cups a handful of cherished water. His smoky breath fanned toward her as he kissed her neck and shoulders. He eased her back onto the pilled spread and tugged off her wet suit, then yanked off his trunks. Kneeling above her, he stroked the length and breadth of her body. His effortless erection broke her heart. She didn't touch him. She had nothing to give. When he finally tried to enter her, he was just clumsy enough for her to have to help. She was taken aback by how gentle he was. The poor boy couldn't hold out, but, in truth, neither could she. He collapsed on top of her, kissing her face and breasts.

"I could fall in love with you," he said at length.

"Finster, you hardly even know me." She eased him off her, sat up, and reached into the pocket of her robe. She dug out a cigarette and lit up. "Thomas can't find out about this," she said.

"How would he?"

"I don't know, Finster, but he'd better not."

Like a soldier on his belly, he crawled over and lay his head on her lap, taking in a deep whiff of her. She sat there and let him, partly because she couldn't bear to go back to her room, partly because she couldn't bear to put on her wet bathing suit, partly because she needed to be so shamelessly desired.

"Didn't you like that, Helene, one bit?"

"For God's sake, Finster, please."

She leaned over, picked up his watch on the nightstand, and glanced at its radium green numbers. Sighing loudly, she started to rise but stopped herself. With efficient tenderness, she kissed him on his forehead. He shut his eyes. She could see him luxuriate in the teeniest gesture of kindness. Then she stood up, braced herself, and pulled on her clammy suit.

"You're shivering," he said. "Do you want to take my towel?"

"Thanks, but no thanks, Finster. How would I explain it to Thomas?"

She opened the door, looked back at Finster whose cheek was now mashed against the spot where she'd sat, and headed to the pool. She waded in up to her neck, then plunged under to douse herself in chlorine. Hauling herself out, she slipped on her robe and lit a cigarette, practically swallowing the smoke, like one might pop a breath mint. Shivering, she headed back to her room. Thomas hadn't moved. He lay supine in a sheen of sweat, one hand flung over his eyes, the other crumpled on his chest. She peeled off her sopping suit and sat down on the bamboo chair, drawing up her knees. The chair creaked horribly under her weight, but Thomas didn't stir. She lit another cigarette, but it just made her more nervous, so she put it out, crushing the glow into ashes. Sometime around midnight, she finally crawled into bed, but she stuck to her narrow margin of mattress.

The Vatu caves were a chain of huge, convoluted caverns in the mountains above Baguay.

Sunday morning, Thomas, Helene, and Finster drove there as planned. No one wanted to go, but no one dared say anything. Thomas was tired. Helene thought she might go mad in the company of both men. Finster was disquietingly sober and kept his eyes riveted to the back of Helene's head.

They parked in the cave's paved parking lot. It was as vast as a shopping mall's. There were only two other vehicles—the caretaker's truck, and a squat van with *Paradise Tours* stenciled on its pitted door.

A dozen faded signs in a dozen far-flung languages read, VATU CAVES, THE EIGHTH WONDER OF THE WORLD! A group of pink-kneed tourists were milling around the cave's opening. Thomas thought he recognized the clip and bark of British English.

"Adam?! Adam Finster!" someone shouted, and a grinning Mr. Khan, revealing an abundance of crimson teeth, stepped out from amid the tourists. "What brings you to—" The Indian stopped, recognizing Thomas and Helene. "Mr. and Mem Strauss, what a pleasant surprise!"

"You two know each other?" Thomas asked, looking querulously at Finster.

"Adam lives in our village. He is my main man," Mr. Khan said, laughing, giving Finster the high five.

"I taught him that," Finster said.

"Don't believe him, Mr. Strauss, I learned that from American movies."

Helene stepped into the shade and leaned against a shaggy palm.

"Mem Strauss, have you not adjusted to our beastly heat yet?"

"Not yet," Helene said.

"Be patient. It takes time. I've been in Vanduu for nine years and I still have not adjusted." He laughed again, clasping his palms together as if he was shaking his own hand. "You'll be happy to know the caves are quite cool, Mem Strauss, often chilly. I hope you and Mr. Strauss will join my tour party. After all, a cave is just a cave without its history."

Finster gnawed on his bitten-to-the-quick fingernails and stared at Helene. Thomas watched Finster curiously. Helene said, "We'd love to."

Mr. Khan clapped his hands loudly, then signaled everyone to follow him. *"Vila masuk! Vila masuk!* Be careful, the caves are very dark and slippery."

He shined his flashlight on the bat-guano-splattered floor, then swung it around the dank, dripping limestone walls. Enormous pink stalactites shaped like Chinese temples and beasts hung from the ceiling.

"The creation myth of the Vatu caves is a little racy, ladies and gentlemen. I do not wish to offend anyone, so please bear with me."

He focused the beam on a crude stick drawing of a man with a penis so long that it continued well out of the glow.

"The father of Vanduu was a man with a fifty-foot member."

The light skimmed across the wall and stopped on a sketchy version of Venus on the half shell, only it was a naked boy atop a split coconut.

"One afternoon, he cracked open a coconut and out of the husk a son, Vatu, was born. The boy grew up to be as well-endowed as his father. When Vatu was playing in the jungle one day, he saw a woman walking up the path. He hailed her, saying, *'Wo omung mitakuku yoku,'* which means, Hullo, sweetheart, I would like to exchange nibbling of eyelashes. The woman said, *'O gala ikwani,'* which means, Nothing doing. Vatu said, *'O kimali kadi kimali yoku'*; in other words, I would like to exchange erotic scratches. The woman laughed and walked away, but Vatu ran ahead, and by means of magic, made a mountain, which covered him, leaving only his penis sticking out. The woman met her sisters along the path and they came upon this intriguing object sticking out of the earth, and began to quarrel about to whom it belonged. One after the other, they bestrode it, pulling each other off, each wanting to enjoy it as long as possible. That night, the first woman returned to dig up the object so that she could take it home with her and hide it from her sisters. She dug and dug, but Vatu's penis was so long, she never reached the boy. And she died of thirst and starvation making the Vatu caves."

Mr. Khan aimed his flashlight into a gaping black hole and signaled everyone to follow him. The passage was low and narrow. Helictites, like lacy icicles, dripped from the ceiling. He stopped and gathered everyone around him, then pointed his beam upward. The cavity opened up into a vast chamber; the ceiling was over thirty feet high.

"This chamber is called Gua Omung, Love Grotto. The natives believed that it was Vatu's home. It was taboo to enter it until the war came and the Japanese arrived. The soldiers kidnapped whole villages of men, women, and children, and put them into forced labor. Thousands died of starvation and disease. Many perished from fear alone. Those who were lucky escaped to the caves. They lived in here for months, eating bats."

He aimed his beam into a deep recess whose walls began to writhe, as if they were breathing. A subliminal rumbling vibrated through the chamber.

"Over ten thousand bats live in these caves."

The beam dropped down to reveal a pool of crystalline water, a charred pit, and a rusted bazooka.

"Eventually, the Japanese found the caves and forced the natives back into labor camps. By the time the Americans arrived, only a quarter of the population was still alive, and they were sick and dying. The Americans surrounded the island with ships. For one solid week, they bombarded everything—villages, barracks, camps—trying to kill as many Japanese as possible before they came ashore. But the Japanese had entrenched themselves in the caves. Over fifteen hundred troops were packed in here, shoulder to shoulder, weapon to weapon. The rest hid in the mountains. On the first day of the American landing, three thousand marines were killed. Four thousand Japanese also lost their lives, and no one counted how many islanders. The battle lasted two and a half months, and was one of the bloodiest in the Pacific. When it was over, the Americans hurried on to the Philippines, not even bothering to set up a base here. The few Japanese soldiers who were left evaded capture by burrowing deep into the caves. The tunnels are miles long, often only a couple of feet high. A man would have to live on his belly, like a lizard, in total darkness. When the war ended, the stragglers were rounded up and shipped home, except for one soldier. He did not know the war had ended, and he lived on in the caves for three more years.

"The native women sometimes spied him when they were planting taro near the cave's mouth, and rumors arose that Vatu had returned. In native folklore, Vatu often snuck up on the women as they planted taro, allowing his long member to snake along the ground and enter the women as they bent over. Whenever an unmarried woman became pregnant, she would claim Vatu was the father. If the baby was a boy and well-endowed, the village accepted her story.

"Eventually, it was the women who captured the soldier, now no more than a living skeleton, and brought him back to their village. The natives could have taken revenge—after all, they had lost so many and so much—but they did not. They fed him and cared for him until he was sent back to Japan.

"I met the gentleman, Mr. Yamamoto, last year on the fiftieth anniversary of the war's end. He was the only Japanese soldier to return to Vanduu. He said the old natives remembered him and were very kind, but the American veterans shunned him. Who can blame the Americans? So many boys were killed. When I asked Mr. Yamamoto if he would like to visit the caves, he politely declined. He said he could no longer bear darkness.

"Now, of course, ten thousand tourists visit our caves every year. The Love Grotto is particularly popular with Japanese honeymooners. Back at the van, I have many excellent picture postcards of Love Grotto and all the other splendors of the Vatu caves for sale. Unfortunately, photos are not permitted in the caverns. The flashbulbs disturb the bats, and we would not want ten thousand bats getting angry at us, would we?" He laughed, then pointed his flashlight up, casting the ceiling in concentric halos. "This is as far as we are allowed to venture for safety reasons. There are still many unexploded shells hidden in these tunnels. But to give you an idea of what it's like to exist in total darkness, I will turn off my torch for one minute."

Everything vanished.

Thomas was stunned by the solidity of the darkness. It was flat, as if the world had lost dimension along with light. He held up his hand, inches from his eyes (he could feel his breath on his palm), but he saw nothing. He turned his head left, then right, but the only sensory change was a crick in his neck. A sense of being bodiless overtook him, and he felt, for the first time in days, calm. He closed his eyes to see if the darkness mimicked sleep, and a tincture of panic seeped in. It didn't mimic sleep. The darkness didn't mimic that comfort at all. Suddenly he couldn't bear to open his eyes again, he couldn't bear to see the same blackness on both sides of his lids—nothing within, nothing without—but he couldn't stop himself from looking. He stared at the spot where Helene had just been. She'd been right beside him, but now that reality seemed so beside the point. He was like a man trapped in an overturned boat knowing that air is just on the other side of the hull. He was suffocating, but that implied a corporeal being, a being with lungs and limbs, and he felt like a waft of consciousness, if even that. He jammed his palms against his lids, stimulating shots of color, and waited for the darkness to end.

Helene hadn't been listening to a single word Mr. Khan said, and she was shocked to find herself in total darkness. But the darkness came as a relief. She'd been sandwiched between Thomas and Finster, with both men constantly watching her, and she didn't think she could take it much longer. She stepped backward into the void, not caring if she trod on some tourist's toes. She needed to get away for a moment so that she could think clearly, but the darkness had the same moiling, roiling effect as insomnia, and her thoughts began spinning around and around, like socks in a washing machine. She couldn't believe she'd slept with that stupid boy. She had to get rid of him. As soon as she and Thomas got back to the hotel, they'd check out and disappear. They lost Finster before, they'd do it again. Then they'd go home. But the thought of going home with Thomas saddened her, because now, anyplace they went, anyplace they were, would be permeated not just with illness, but with petty, needless duplicity, too. What if Finster says something to Thomas? What if that stupid boy says something to him? I'll have to get rid of him myself, she thought. She heard someone cough. It sounded grotesquely loud, like an overheard cough through a paper-thin wall of a cheap hotel in the middle of the night. I'm going to go out of my mind if I don't get rid of him today. For a moment, in the solid darkness, she became confused about which man she was getting rid of. Suddenly she ached to get back to Thomas's side, but she didn't know where he was.

Finster was convinced that he was brushing up against Helene in the dark. He was sure he could smell her shampoo, though the stench of bat shit humbled all else. They hadn't had a chance to be alone all morning, and he was aching. He inched closer, nudging the rim of his rubber flip-flops against her bare ankle. He felt something soft and fleeting grace his wrist. The hem of her tank top? The down of her arm? There was something unbearably sexy about the outer-space blackness, the steam of the doltish crowd, and the fact that he could still taste her on his hands. He brought his fingers up to his face and took a deep whiff.

Then the light popped on.

Thomas returned to his corporeal being, Helene found herself on the outskirts of the crowd, and Finster was flush against an English matron with sun-fried skin and two buckteeth shaped like matching tombstones. The woman looked at Finster in abject disgust.

On the drive back, no one spoke. Thomas drove, Finster sat in the rear, Helene cranked down her window and stuck her head out to let the rush of air hypnotize her, the way a dog does. She tried to focus on the sun, the skidding wind, the hiss of tires, but now and again a slip of a thought crept in, and it was always the same.

If she didn't get rid of that boy, she'd go mad.

At the hotel, Finster followed her into the lobby, trying to catch her eye, but she ignored him. She stuck as close to Thomas as possible, looping her arm through his as they walked to their bungalow. The instant they were alone, she said they had to pack up and leave, *today*.

Thomas sat down on the bed and rubbed his temples with the heels of his hands. "Where are we going now, Helene?"

"Home."

"It's not that simple." He went over the difficult logistics with her: They had to return the car to Mr. Khan in the village, they had to arrange for transportation to Minaphor, they had to find out if they could even get airplane tickets back to New York on this short notice.

"Fine. Then you stay in this hellhole."

She walked out, slamming the door behind her. Finster was lurking behind their bungalow.

"Helene, I've got to talk to you."

"Are you nuts? Not here."

She started down the path in the opposite direction of the lobby.

"Helene, wait. I need to talk to you."

"There's nothing to say, Finster. We fucked. Done, over, forgotten."

"I think I'm in love with you."

"Oh, God, Finster, please, you're not in love with me. You've been smoking too much dope."

"I haven't had a hit all day."

"Then maybe you should have one." She hurried on, but the path soon petered out, ending in a heap of junk covered with lichens.

"Please, Helene." Finster caught up with her and touched her bare shoulder, caressing it with his fingertips. "Meet me in my bungalow tonight, just to talk, I swear."

She shot him a look of weary exasperation, then walked back to the room. Thomas was waiting by the window, absently toying with the blinds. "We need to talk, Helene," he said.

"I'm not talking to anyone right now." She flopped onto the bed and curled up, trying to ignore him, but he sat down beside her. The bounce of him on the mattress made her feel as if she were being catapulted off solid ground.

"Do you have to sit so close? I can't breathe."

He looked at her with tenderness and terror, and she slammed her eyes shut. "I need to be alone," she said.

"What does that mean, Helene?"

She wasn't sure. "It means exactly what it means."

"Are you saying you want to be alone right now? Or are you saying you want to be alone from now on?"

"I don't know," she said. She opened her eyes and studied the wall beside her, the finger marks and squashed mosquitoes. "Why can't you just take the car back to Mr. Khan's and I'll meet you there in a day or two."

"That's not possible, Helene. You can't travel alone in this country."

"I've traveled alone a zillion times, Thomas. I've lived in every goddamn hovel in every goddamn country you've done fieldwork in. I visited you in your bloody Amazon, for Christ's sake. How do you think I got there?"

"I don't know Vanduu."

"It doesn't matter what *you* know, Thomas. That's not the point. The point is—" She wasn't sure what the point was. "The point is, *I need to be alone.*" She mashed her face into the pillow and a sob came up, clearing the passage for others. "You won't even touch me."

"That's not true." He touched her cheek with infinite delicacy.

"That doesn't count."

"What counts, Helene?"

She could feel the mattress buck, then sag. She knew he was getting up. She slowly raised her head.

"It's one thing that you can't fuck me, Thomas, but it's another that you don't want to."

He stopped at the end of their bed. When he turned around, his face reflected such cold composure, stretched over such breathtaking pain, that it stunned her. "You have no idea what you're talking about," he said. His voice sounded strangled and distant, as if it were coming from an adjacent room. He gave a hard, sharp shake of his head, like a man trying to release an earful of water. "What do you want from me, Helene?"

"I want us to be like we were before."

"It's not going to happen."

"How do you know? Why are you so fucking sure of everything all the time?"

"I'm not sure of anything anymore, Helene."

"I don't know who you are. Why don't you come back?"

"Please don't say that." He sank onto the bed and cradled his head in his hands. She knew he was crying. For some inexplicable reason, by making him as miserable as she felt, she was able to calm down. She sat up, leaned over, and placed her lips on the back of his head. She lifted his hands off his face and kissed both palms. She held his head, as one holds the weight of a medicine ball, and laid it on her lap. "I just need to be by myself for a couple of days, Thomas. Then we'll go home."

With great reluctance, Thomas finally agreed to take the car back to Mr. Khan's in the morning. Helene would join him there in two days, when a direct, first-class bus left Baguay for the village. In the meantime, to expedite their return home, Thomas would hire Mr. Khan to make their travel arrangements through Paradise Tours. If everything worked out as planned, they'd be ready to leave Vanduu the instant Helene got to the village.

That evening, they dined in strained silence at a roadside food stall, then went to bed early. Around nine, Finster tapped on their door, but they ignored him. In all their years together, they'd rarely been able to sleep in each other's arms. Even before Thomas got sick, he'd slept like a feverish man, and Helene, a human seismograph, would awaken to his every jerk and toss. But tonight, they lay fastened together, spoon fashion. She could feel his hot breath break over the back of her neck. She had no idea what their being separated for two days could possibly accomplish, save for the fact that she could finally get rid of Finster, and she could hardly explain *that* to Thomas. To calm herself down and fall asleep, she went over their plans—*her plans*—in niggling detail, as other people count sheep, or tally up baseball scores, or add up ex-lovers. Thomas would leave in the morning and she would get rid of Finster. Thomas would return the car to the village and she would join him there later. He would secure the bus tickets to the airport in Minaphor and she would make sure they had enough bottled water and food to eat on the way. He would buy the airplane tickets and she would see to the luggage. He would take the aisle seat and she would take the center. He would hail the cab at JFK and she would collect the suitcases. He would collapse in his armchair at home and she would stare out the window. He would get sicker and sicker and she would spend day after day in numb panic. He would die in bed at home and she would be left with his books and his papers and the enigma of what their life, with its glut of love and its paltry mercy, had been all about.

Early the next morning, while Thomas went to buy gas, Helene packed his things, and most of her own, save for a change of underwear, an extra pair of shorts, a tank top, and her toothbrush. At the last minute, she slipped her passport into the suitcase as well, just in case he should need it to finalize the airline ticket purchase. The last thing they wanted was to get stuck in one of Mr. Khan's suffocating rooms for an extra night, while copies of her passport were sent to whatever paranoid security men run this part of the world. She lugged the suitcases out to the parking lot.

Thomas was waiting in the idling car, head bowed, studying Mr. Khan's map, or pretending to study it. When he looked up at her, his face was a meld of consternation and dread. "Helene, this is insane."

She fiddled with the antenna: She bent it back like a bow. "Please, let's not argue anymore," she said. She picked up the suitcases and hoisted them into the trunk. When she came back, Thomas was picking at the rubber window gutter. Had he just grasped her hand, had he touched her in any way, she would have forgotten this madness and climbed in beside him. But he didn't stop picking at the window gutter. She lightly touched his cheek: She didn't caress it, she simply pressed her hand against it. "Promise me you'll pull over and rest if you feel tired?"

"For God's sake, Helene, I can drive a fucking car."

She withdrew her hand.

"You should probably leave before it gets too hot," she said.

"I probably should."

"I'll see you in a couple of days."

They did not kiss good-bye.

Two miles out of Baguay, the road to the village veered off the main highway, then zigzagged into a shadowy valley hemmed in by spiky green ridges. For the first half hour or so, Thomas debated whether or not to turn back, but when he tried to imagine what he and Helene would say—all those clipped repetitions and wooden silences—the idea seemed as pointless as going on. He studied the road. A sluggish black stream crossed under it, and sometimes over it, and the road's surface was as pocked and cratered as the moon's.

Swerving left, then right, he tried to avoid the holes, but he couldn't concentrate, and the car clunked and joggled along.

At the first tin town, he stopped to get something to eat and drink, but the little tin grocery store only sold Spam, Pringles, and orange soda pop in plastic bottles the size of aquariums.

He drove on. The sun had grown enormous, cleaving the world into shadow and glare, black and white, soot and fire. An ink-black goat flashed by with a molten bell. The palm trunks stood like charred pilings, the fronds dripped like jewel-fires. Squinting into the rush and pulse, he forced himself to think about nothing, but now and again, a snippet of his and Helene's last argument welled up, like a dead radio that crackles to life.

He passed a billboard advertising *Baywatch*. The crew was standing fifteen feet tall, shoulder to bare, tanned, impeccable shoulder.

The text was Vanduuan, but the gist was clear: Nothing would harm these blond gods and goddesses, not riptide or undertow or illness or age. And for some reason, this ridiculous ad made the inevitable demise of his marriage feel real.

Another tin town streaked by. Women and children were squatting around a drainage ditch, shamelessly relieving themselves. As they wavered away in the rising heat, he distinctly heard, in the inmost chamber of his ear, Helene say, "I need to be alone, Thomas!"

He snapped on the radio to distract himself, but deep in the valley, there was only static, punctuated by a sporadic nasal drone he vaguely recognized as singing. Sometimes the voice reached octaves of pure joy or pitched hysteria, he couldn't tell which, but mostly it sounded like whining.

Experience told him that he was on the brink of a panic attack. He took a couple of measured breaths. He could feel the sun on his arm, the icy pulse of the air conditioner on his throat, but neither felt tonic or soothing. More than anything, he wanted to talk to Helene. He thought if he could just speak to her, he might catch his breath. He pulled onto the shoulder of the road, waited for a flatbed to roll by, then turned around and started back to Baguay.

He drove a mile or two before he came to a fork. He vaguely remembered having veered left at this point, but he wasn't sure. The map lay open on the passenger seat. In the unremitting sunlight, he could barely read it, save for the tourist sights, which were drawn big and cartoonish, as if one might be able to discern them from afar, like mountain peaks. The mapmaker, probably Mr. Khan himself, had eliminated anything confusing—extra roads, forks, shantytowns, junk heaps—so that single, bold-faced lines ran straight through paradise, from one tourist sight to another, from the Vatu caves to Motel Paradise. Thomas crumpled up the map and threw it on the floor.

He drove up the left fork for a hundred yards. It looked very familiar, but just to make sure, he doubled back and drove up the right one. It looked equally familiar. He rubbed his temples with the heels of his hands, then rested his brow against the steering wheel. He knew he shouldn't go back to Helene right now, that it would only make matters worse. Once again, he turned around and headed toward Mr. Khan's.

The sun was directly overhead now, scoring hot spots on the hood. They flared and shriveled, quivered and imploded, annoying him to the point of anguish. He focused on the scenery. For the first mile or so, he recognized the landmarks, if one could call them landmarks—the water buffalo whose gray hide looked like peeling wallpaper, the farm teeming with scrawny pigs, the burnt shack by the mini-swamp. But even after he passed the point at which he'd turned around, the landscape remained weirdly familiar.

He chalked it up to the fact that one equatorial road was hardly distinguishable from another, but even as he thought that, he knew it wasn't true. He suspected that those momentary global shifts that had plagued him for weeks had simply widened to include scrawny pigs, burnt shacks, lugubrious water buffaloes, that he could have been, and was, driving down a myriad of roads at once—the highway out of Brasília, the lumber road near Iquitos, the dirt trek between Macapá and Obidos, even the gravel road to his boyhood house in Gowanda, New York—and this both terrified and exhilarated him. The world had become *that* familiar.

The car's air conditioner begun to sputter. The breeze that reached him was tepid and lulling. The trees rushed at him in achromatic grays, not unlike the halogen sensation of memory itself, and this calmed him to the point of grogginess.

A lumber truck thundered by. In the buck of its wake, he thought he heard a hunk of wood smack his bumper. But the sound was a little more pliant, a little more malleable than wood, and he figured he might have hit another pig, or a dog. He had no intention of stopping this time. He goosed the gas pedal before glancing back in the rearview mirror.

Angled in the smudged glass, a little girl crouched over a hurt animal, trying to comfort it. He knew it was a girl because she was wearing a white head scarf that knocked about in the wind. Then it dawned on him that she was Muslim, and she would not touch a pig or a dog, that there was no creature beneath her.

He skidded to a stop and stepped out of the car.

A woman toting an enormous bundle of crooked sticks came out of the jungle, screamed, dropped the bundle, ran and knelt over the child.

He felt a jolt of something acidic, but it didn't yet register as horror. Horror would feel insufferable, dense, weighty as ingots or pig iron, and he felt light-headed, unmoored, etherized.

He started walking, then running toward them. The woman, shrouded in a flowered shawl, had balled herself over the girl. Only her face and sandaled feet were visible. The girl, or what Thomas could see of her, lay still.

He crouched down to see if he could stir her back to consciousness by shaking her. He actually pushed the woman aside to get to her, and as he did so, the woman's shocked countenance imploded into a gash of loss so immense and irreparable that Thomas couldn't take its measure.

He looked at the child; it was so incomprehensibly apparent that she was dead—her body lay as twisted as a French curve—that when he finally touched her, he was stunned to find her arm still warm.

He turned to the woman, not for forgiveness—forgiveness was out of the question—but for collusion, as if the two of them could band together to wring or shake or rattle the body into breathing.

But the woman would not look at him.

He stood up to summon help from the murmur of voices he heard behind him, and a rock hit the side of his head. For a moment, he thought it was a new, more appropriate sensation of grief. He touched the spot. His hand came back blotted with blood. In his dazed state, he assumed it was the child's blood, that somehow it had flown up off the child's body to coat his hands. Another rock caromed off his shoulder.

A dozen men and women stood or squatted on the blistering asphalt. Two of the women wore traditional shawls, but the others were tented in flapping muumuus. None of them appeared to be the ones lobbing rocks.

"Please let me take her to the hospital in my car. Maybe there's still something that can be done," Thomas said, but even as he said it, the futility of it crushed him.

No one responded. The only sound came from the woman holding the child. She made a sibilant, gurgling noise, like someone gargling without water.

Another stone struck his back, bouncing off his belt. He turned around and saw three mud-flecked teenage boys. One wore a peci, but the other two sported baseball caps and T-shirts that said *Holy Commando* and *Take the Pepsi Challenge.* The smallest of the three picked up a rock, then brazenly positioned it in his grip, like a pitcher does when preparing to throw a curve ball.

"Does anyone speak English?" Thomas asked the adults. "Cakap Inggeris? Please let me take her to the hospital." Looking from one face to another—veiled, foreign, wrinkled as bark, expressionless as a skillet—he couldn't tell whether they understood him or not.

He started to crouch down over the child again, but a farmer stepped forward and pushed him away. A woman unpinned her shawl and put it over the child's face, but the woman holding the child shook her head furiously and tore it off.

Thomas looked at the face—chalky, flaccid, absurdly young. Two olive-size flies were already perched on the bottom lip.

A rock struck his brow this time and left him reeling. He stumbled backward, then squatted down, half-shielding, half-cupping his head in his hands, all the while gulping down stunted, wheezing breaths. When he could focus again, he saw the boys goading one another on. He stood up and slowly began walking backward toward the car.

The boys followed, picking up and chucking an occasional stone. These were only pinging warnings. The stones were tiny, and of the same flat, blunted variety that suburbanites mix with cement to make decorative patios.

The car was standing on the jungle-clotted shoulder, its tires crushing monster ferns, its door open like a wing. Thomas sat down on the front seat, on the searing vinyl, and began searching for the keys. He checked the ignition, then rooted his hands in his pant pockets, but all he felt were coins. He bent forward, flattening himself against the steering wheel, and reached down to blindly palpate the floor, the rubber mat, under the seat, the crevice between the cushions, the plastic terrain around the gear shift. The door was open and, hanging on to the steering wheel, he leaned out to scour the thick, tangled foliage for where he might have dropped them.

A stone struck him flat on the cranium, and for a moment, he saw the inkling of a firmament.

He sat up, cradling his head, and stared at the boys. He said, as loudly and clearly as possible, "For God's sake, I'm going to try and bring back *help*!"

A rock glanced off the roof and he drew himself inside and slammed the door.

His head was burning, as if someone was filling it with hot wax. He tried to think where he might have put the keys, but he couldn't think. Touching his head, he felt a Ping-Pong–size protuberance above his left ear, a gash at the base of his skull, a searing welt where the last stone had clobbered him. He rested his temple, the only spot that didn't throb, against the steering wheel. Under the noon sun, the plastic felt like a wheel of fire.

Two farmers walked over to join the boys, and for a moment, Thomas thought they were going to charge the car and rock it, rock it till they tipped it over and crushed him. But the farmers merely squatted on the pavement, while now and again, one of the boys lobbed a rock at the car. One pinged off the trunk, another shattered the rear windshield, a third cracked the front one.

The temperature inside the car was growing hotter by the second. He cracked open the window for a breath of air, but a volley of stones pelted the glass. He quickly rolled it up again and shut his eyes. He heard dogs, with voices as shrill as Kate Smith, wailing behind him. When he looked back to see what was happening with the child, all he could make out, in the shattered glass, was a kaleidoscope of colored muumuus.

The car was so hot now that whenever he took a breath, he felt as if he was scalding his lungs. He actually had to sip the air, as one sips hot tea. He passed out for a moment, only to awaken in a state of such panic that he flung open the door. The boys were waiting with their rocks, but they didn't need to throw them this time. Thomas merely looked at their seething stances and obediently returned to his oven. He touched his face. It was as dry as plastic. He wasn't even sweating anymore. All the sweat had been blotted out of him and flashed away.

A truck, or at least a shimmer of steel and a plume of diesel fumes, appeared on the horizon. Thomas pushed down on his horn with all his strength and blasted it. The sound was eerily human and seemed to be coming from his own chest, but the truck barreled by, braking beside the body. He couldn't see what was going on, but he could hear the truck's rumbling engine. After a while, he heard the release of air brakes, and the enormous steel shape glided away.

He closed his eyes and waited for help. He was sure the truck driver would bring back help, if not for him, at least for the girl. He fell asleep and dreamt that his feet were being anointed with the cool, gummy sap of an aloe plant, that the sap held the mysterious powers of dry ice and blue ether. When he came to, the delectable sensation of cold remained. It was moving up his leg at benumbing speed. He surmised, incorrectly, that he was going into shock, when in reality, the fragile vessel beneath the contusion over his left ear had begun rupturing like a water main, spilling blood into his brain, blotting out his life neuron by neuron. He lost the remaining sensation in his right leg and the use of his right hand—the fingers felt, in the abominable heat, as if they'd been transmuted into icicles. He lost feeling in his lips and tongue, and weirdly, his ability to name things—car, man, sun. He lost the reason for his being here, on this particular road, at this particular hour, and he lost his desire to be anywhere else. On the back of his closed lids was a pattern no less intricate than a kaleidoscope, and he knew he was about to fall into its center and lose the essence of what it was to be Thomas. He fought his way back to momentary cognizance. And just before he lost the vital pathway between his brain and his heart, he opened his left eye (he'd lost the use of his right one), saw the shattered windshield, and thought, So this is what it's like to be encased in ice.

Part Two

These were the facts, or the facts as Finster gleaned them. The old man was dead. Heart attack, according to the authorities. The "murdered" child was Aisha Mustakim, the seven-year-old daughter of Muhammad Mustakim. (Her schoolbook picture graced the front page of the *Vanduuan Times* for three days.)

Helene was being sought for questioning. She was accused of fleeing the scene. Her passport and suitcases were found in the car. An eyewitness claimed he'd seen a white woman run into the jungle. Finster knew that last part wasn't true because on the morning of the accident, he was spying on Helene through her window at the Vatu Chalets, trying to figure out how to get her to sleep with him again.

These were the rumors, or the rumors that reached Finster's ear. That Helene had been driving, and the old man only took the fall. That they were both drunk. That Thomas was CIA (his stamped-to-the-gills passport troubled officials). That Helene was CIA. That they'd accidentally struck the child while scouting Vanduu's back country for potential locations to build a secret U.S. military base. That they both tried to flee the scene, but a couple of farm boys stopped Thomas with rocks. That the child had been murdered for her transplantable organs, which were to have been flash-frozen and shipped to America. (This last rumor only whirled around for a couple hours—even the most rabid Vanduuan xenophobe finally realized that no one, not even a callous American businessman, would harvest body parts by plowing into the donor at thirty miles per hour with a rented Toyota.)

Finster was back in his village after a hellish three days of following every minuscule lead in search of Helene. She'd disappeared the day of the accident.

He lay adrift in his Quonset hut on a hammock that he shared with his dogs. One had her rump on his chest, the other was voraciously licking his bare feet. As ashamed as Finster was to admit it, her rough tongue felt divinely sexy. He was skimming the newspaper for any new clues to the case. The story changed almost daily, stoked by uncorroborated rumors and the continued fugitive status of Helene. Today a demonstration was being kicked off in the capital for the four Vanduuans who had died this year alone at the hands of foreigners—one strangled bar girl, one shot karaoke girl, a maid who'd been raped and stabbed by her Minaphorian employer, and the child. So far, not one foreigner had been arrested.

Finster flipped the paper over and read "Today's Thought," a little Seventh-Day Adventist proverb at the bottom of the page:

> *As a dog returns to its vomit, so a fool repeats his folly. (Proverbs 26:11)*

A mini-sermon went with it.

> *Fools don't learn from their mistakes; instead they get locked into distasteful and disgusting habits.*

Finster plucked out a roach, lit up, and tried to figure out what to do next. He was desperate to find Helene. He knew she was still in Vanduu, probably petrified, most likely in shock. She couldn't have gotten out. The borders had been shut down.

Nudging his dogs off the hammock, he took another drag, then scoured his memory of the last few days to see if he'd overlooked some place she might have gone that he hadn't thought of before.

His recollections were tinged in the Day-Glo colors of TCP. Finster believed the drug gave memory an extra dimension, an otherworldly afterglow, a lingering shadow he might not be able to follow otherwise.

On the morning in question, the morning of the accident, he awoke bleary-eyed, having spent the night waiting for Helene to show up at his door. But she never showed up. Through the Vatu Chalets' poor excuse for curtains—an ancient sarong stapled to a wooden dowl—he saw her comely silhouette lugging suitcases out to the car. Sitting up with a jolt, he was about to throw on his Hawaiian trunks and run out when he noticed something peculiar in the way she and Thomas were behaving—they weren't exactly looking at each other. He hung back and waited. Seconds later, Thomas drove off alone, leaving Helene in the middle of the crushed-coral parking lot, standing on her own tiny shadow.

He pulled on his trunks, slipped outside, and secretly dogged her back to her bungalow. He loitered outside her window, concealed in shrubbery, tempted beyond all measure to tap on the glass, but something in her bearing—the angle of her head, the steely tendons in her neck—made him know that he should give her wide berth. But he didn't leave. He was totally intoxicated with her.

He watched her brush out her hair, a sleep-crimped pandemonium of russet and brown. Holding the brush like one grips a ball-peen hammer, she swung furiously at the clumps, whereas, had he been given the task, he would have gladly sorted through and separated each woolly knot with his fingers.

Without warning, she suddenly threw the brush onto the bed and peeled off her T-shirt. Finster heard his own blood banging in his ears. Sniffing the T-shirt with disgust, she used it to mop up under her arms before chucking it onto the floor. Finster would have paid dearly for that T-shirt.

When she finally turned around, he saw that she was crying. Normally, Finster would make his move at this point. He believed a woman's tears were the perfect moment for seduction, an excuse to comfort and console with roving hands. But as he watched Helene, he felt a subliminal, mounting pressure, a tiny eruption of compassion, hinting at something enormous beneath it. She cried with pinched and swallowed jerks, as if she was in physical pain, and as he studied her, he was in pain, too.

"Mistah Finstah!"

He reeled around just in time to see one of his customers, a bowlegged, barrel-shaped chief from a podunk kampung, shouting to him from the stone path. Finster bolted toward him, making shushing gestures.

The old chief had just trekked nine miles through the jungle to buy three vials of perfume. Though polygamy was officially banned, it was widely practiced, and the chief was marrying his third wife, a thirteen-year-old virgin, the following week. Finster quickly ushered him into his bungalow and tried to hasten the sale, but the old chief was in no rush to walk back. He sat down on Finster's floor and asked for a glass of water. He took out a clump of betel nuts and insisted Finster join him. He chewed on his nut as slowly and thoroughly as a cow chews cud. After spitting an endless red stream into the hotel's wicker wastebasket, he wanted Finster to once again explain the magic of his perfume.

Crazed to get back to Helene, Finster reeled off his spiel with the rapidity of an auctioneer, then finally led the chief out. By the time he got back to Helene's bungalow, she was gone.

The door was ajar, so Finster walked in, not quite sure what he was looking for. The only hint of her having been there was a balled-up wad of tissue on a dented pillow, a Club A-Go-Go matchbook, and a couple of russet hairs in the sink.

Finster hurried to the front desk and interrogated the clerk. Did the white woman check out?

The boy was chomping on a huge wad of betel and had to answer Finster's queries with the facial tics that islanders employ when their mouths are gorged with nut. Eyebrows up for yes. Eyebrows motionless for no.

The clerk's eyebrows lifted.

How long ago?

The clerk shrugged noncommittally.

Did her husband come back for her?

The clerk again shrugged noncommittally.

Did she say where she was going?

The clerk's furry eyebrows remained motionless.

Finster groaned, then sat down on the lobby's front step and tried to think. She might have walked into Baguay, but he doubted it. Why would she go there? More than likely, Thomas had picked her up. More than likely, they were on their way to Kuantong or Minaphor. More than likely, they were headed home. The thought of not seeing Helene again left Finster in a stunned panic.

He started walking into town along the shoulder of the highway, barely stepping over the vendor's blankets with their meager displays of hairy rambutans, orange pop bottles, and knock-off Nikes bunched on poles like bananas.

Whenever he heard a car in the distance, he'd look up to scrutinize the approaching vehicle with ludicrous hope, only to see a Sikh in a Q-Tip–shaped turban, or a horde of Vanduuans shoehorned into a Minaphorian sedan.

By the time he got to town, he'd decided to get drunk. Baguay was almost entirely dry. Between the Mormons, the SDAs, and the Muslims, most of the bars had shut down. He headed across town, past the crumbling grandeur of the colonial district, to the spanking-new mini-mall-size Chinatown. The restaurants there sold beer. Plopping down on a plastic chair in a lantern and linoleum storefront, he ordered a Tsingtau, knocked it back, then ordered another. A dozen glassy-eyed Vanduuans were also knocking back beers. Finster spent the afternoon getting blottoed, watching the Chinese owner's extended family peel and pop a hillock of snow peas.

Around four, a truck driver came in, sat down at a beer-laden table, and told the other Vanduuans about a Muslim girl who had just been killed. The way the driver heard it, the child had been killed by two foreigners, Americans. They'd caught one, a *babi vaduk,* but the other, a *dim-dim boru,* got away.

As blottoed as Finster was, he did a quick translation—pig grandfather and white whore. He watched the Chinese family's facial expressions roll up and vanish. Though they'd probably been in Vanduu three generations, any hint of trouble, and they were on as shaky a ground as Finster.

The truck driver said the child had been struck down by the Americans' rented car and that the Americans had tried to flee. When a couple of farmers finally captured the *vaduk,* the old pig had dropped dead of a heart attack. No one actually saw the woman, but the police found her passport in the car. That, at least, was what the truck driver heard from another truck driver, who had heard it from a third truck driver who had been there.

Finster ordered a fresh round of beers for the driver and his pals, then asked where and when it happened.

The driver asked Finster if he was a *dim-dim* American.

"Dim-dim Californian," Finster said, grinning. *"Dim-dim Baywatch."* He was blitzed.

The driver laughed, then told Finster that the "murder" had taken place around eleven, seventy-eight kilometers west of Baguay on the road to Pan'uu, Finster's village.

Finster shoved a wad of American dollars under his sweating, half-finished beer, seesawed outside, felt the pitch and swell of nauseating heat, reeled toward the curb, clung to an arc lamp, then hunkered over the betel-bespattered gutter and retched like a dog.

When he finally looked up, he was seeing sextuple. Across the street in the window of the Hang Lung appliance store was a pyramid of round-shouldered TV's. Six black-and-white Vanduuan newscasters were talking into six black-and-white ball microphones with six black-and-white, blown-up passport photos of Helene behind them.

Finster rubbed his eyes and crossed the street. It was not a good likeness. She looked haggard and fierce, with a raised USA seal, like a rash, across her cheek. He stepped into the ice-cold store just long enough to crank up the volume on a set and hear that she was still at large. Cupping his splitting head, he lumbered back out, found a shady bench, and paid two urchins to fetch him mineral water, aspirin, and tutti-fruiti Chiclets.

He downed the water for electrolytes, the aspirin for pain, and chomped the Chiclets to mask the swampy taste in his mouth. Then he did some quick calculations. If the accident happened at eleven, or thereabouts—Vanduuan time was a tad elastic—there was no way that Helene could have been in the car. Finster had been spying on her until at least nine-thirty. The road between Baguay and the village was a cratered mess. Unless Thomas drove like Mario Andretti, he couldn't have come back for her and still made the seventy-odd kilometers by eleven. Dizzying possibilities trod across Finster's sotted brain. There was as good a chance as any that Helene was still in Baguay. He stood up, but something else nagged at him, something weighty just beyond the margin of his legible thoughts. He vaguely recalled the driver saying that something fatal had happened to the *vaduk,* and it finally hit him that Thomas was dead.

He sat down. The bracing realization sobered him. He felt terrible. He'd truly admired the man, even looked up to him. He sat for a minute in respectful silence, then bolted up to search for Helene.

She probably didn't have a clue as to what had happened, probably thought Thomas was still coming back for her. He checked the souvenir shops along the main drag, the two, three temples open to tourists, the upscale eateries in the downtown hotels. He even inquired at the front desks in case she and Thomas had decided to move without telling him. Finally, in a leap of illogic, he jogged along the streets just asking people if they'd seen her. When nothing panned out, he headed to the bus depot, a sole kiosk on a dirt lot, and queried the Vanduuan ticket lady as to whether or not she'd seen a white woman. A bus was the only way out of Baguay. He described Helene in ridiculous detail—"russet hair, mole on cheek"—but the woman merely shrugged noncommittally, then sat down in her coffin-size kiosk and began preparing betel. A couple of Chinese trishaw drivers were smoking cheroot in the shadow of a rusted bus shell. Finster trotted over and asked them if they'd seen a white lady get on a bus. He flashed an American five. One of the drivers glanced around, then whispered that he might have seen a young mem with red hair get on a bus around noon. When Finster asked him why he hadn't told that to the police, the man looked at him in outright fear, then quickly pedaled off. Finster walked back to the kiosk. The last spokes of daylight were glancing off the tin walls. Squinting into the raw glare, he read the day's schedule. The noon bus had been a nonstop to the capital. Finster knew there were no other "redheaded young mems" in Baguay. He bought a ticket for the next bus—a fourth-class relic that stopped in every podunk kampung. It left in a half hour. For a moment, Finster debated jogging back to the Chalets to pick up what was left of his perfumes, but decided against it. His head pounded, his eyeballs felt sandblasted, the back of his tongue tasted as if it had grown hair.

When the bus finally pulled out an hour and a half later, Finster was crammed between an enormous old man, who mumbled as he read his dog-eared Bible, and an Indian woman with a baby goat. For some crazed reason, the goat found Finster's Hawaiian trunks irresistible.

A sign over the driver's seat said NO BETEL, but everyone was chomping away anyhow. The outside of the windows were streaked with red spittle.

Finster rested his head on the old man's shoulder and slept.

It was dawn when the bus finally lumbered into the capital. Finster immediately bought the morning paper. The dead child's photo practically covered the front page. She was wearing her school uniform, a white head scarf that cloaked her forehead and ears. Her tiny features, framed in all that billowing whiteness, looked as if they were coming out of a cloud. A half dozen "artitorials"—part article, mostly editorial—covered the case. Finster skimmed the paragraphs about the child and her grieving family, and focused on the accident. So far, the police were calling it a hit-and-run, which in Vanduu meant murder. One reporter seemed irate that Thomas had dared drop dead before he could get his comeuppance. Another blamed the death on Vanduu's ceaseless dependence on tourist dollars. A third proposed the theory that Thomas was part of a secret U.S. State Department contingency sent here to bully Vanduu into becoming an American satellite. There were almost no hard facts to go on, save for the inflexible reality of the child's death, and this only seemed to stoke a frustration that had been smoldering for years.

Two of the articles zeroed in on Helene, and Finster read them with breathless urgency. A farmer from the kampung of Bintan had come forward to claim that a woman of Helene's description had killed his prize pig with her car one week before. A lottery ticket vendor said a white woman with red hair had been in the downtown bus terminal the night before. Both articles gave Helene's bare-bones description, evidently gleaned from her passport, but neither ran her picture.

Finster chucked away the paper and headed to the hotel district. By now, she had to know that they were looking for her, and the hotel district was the only ten square blocks in Vanduu where a tourist might blend in.

He checked the Continental, the Oriental, the International, bribing bellhops for information, but no one had seen Helene. He trudged the teeming alleys, trying the incense-reeking hostels and Chinese rooming houses. A clever person might vanish into one of their Chinese box rooms forever. He made a dozen phone calls, to every hotelier he'd ever glad-handed, hoping that if they saw Helene, they'd call him before the police.

He hailed a pedicab to take him to the U.S. consulate, a windowless office in Vanduu's only skyscraper, then thought better of it. No one there would tell him anything anyhow. The consulate had recently changed hands. The old guard, a savvy, florid-faced Texan named Lucien Parker, had been forcibly retired, and the new attaché, a buzz-cut State Department geek who spewed anagrams as other men spew swear words, hated Finster. At an official party that Finster had crashed last month, the man had referred to him as AMR (American Mercantile Riffraff). Finster told the pedicab driver to take him to Parker's. The old guy had been entrenched in Vanduu since WWII, and had everyone on his payroll, including Finster. Finster supplied him with an occasional bottle of perfume, an occasional Baggie of dope, and whatever info Finster brought back from the boonies. If anyone knew Helene's whereabouts, it would be Parker.

The ex–vice consul's house, a replica of an adobe hacienda fortressed behind a twelve-foot cinder-block fence, was perched atop Vanduu City's highest hill. The iron gates were flanked by machine-gun-toting private guards, most of whom were Finster's customers. They grinned at him and waved him inside. Parker lay adrift on a plastic float in his swimming pool. The pool was shaped like the state of Texas. His eighteen-year-old Filipina girlfriend, Carmela, was listlessly rubbing his huge back with her toy-size hands.

Finster trotted up to the pool's edge and blurted out his queries.

"'Fraid I don't know anything, Adam, 'fraid I've been locked out of the loop this time." Parker waved Carmela away, then slid off the float and waded toward Finster. Rivulets of water ran off his copper scalp. "Have you met the new man in town, the economic attaché? Doesn't look like a potential customer, huh? No, he's a New World Order man—*whatever that means.*"

"You don't know anything?" Finster asked.

"I know the dead man was some sort of academic mucky-muck." Parker rolled his eyes heavenward. "You can imagine how much *that* means in Vanduu." He clumsily hauled his thick bulk onto the tiled decking, then dipped a beefy hand back into the turquoise water and ladled it over his fried neck and shoulders. "'Fraid there's no word on the wife yet, Adam." Peering over his sunglasses, he shot Finster a curious look. "Why all the interest in a professor's wife?" He wrinkled his brow in mock befuddlement. "Can't believe it's patriotism. She looked quite fetching from her passport photo, and the husband was what . . . *my age?*" He clicked his tongue, then wagged a finger at Finster. "You weren't bumping uglies with her, were you, boy?" He loudly clapped his hands and gestured for Carmela to bring them drinks.

"No thanks," Finster said.

"You want to smoke a little peace pipe instead?"

"Not today."

"I do believe I should mark this date on my calendar. Carmela! Bring me my calendar! Today marks the day that Finster refused a hit!"

As soon as Carmela vanished behind the sliding glass door, Parker turned back to Finster. "Listen, no one's going to lift a hand to help the woman. That's the unofficial word. She's OHO, 'on her own,' as

Mr. Prick-Face Attaché says. My opinion: They're going to use her as a bone to throw the mongrel hordes, give the Vanduuans the illusion of sovereignty, while they talk all the old aunties into selling their land so they can secure their fallback position just in case Aquino chucks us out. They've got designs on Vanduu and one little prof's wife is more than expendable. If I were you, and I knew where she was, I'd get her out of here wikki-wikki."

"Thanks, Parker," Finster said, rising to his feet. He started trotting toward the gate.

"Adam!"

Finster reeled around.

"I'd think about getting out, too. Men like you and me, old-time entrepreneurs, we're dinosaurs. Vanduu's about to change, big time, and I don't think you're going to like it. Me, I'm stuck here. What with the house, and my tropical fish collection, and Carmela, and her hive-size family . . . can't quite envision us all dining at the Dairy Queen in El Paso."

Finster climbed back into the waiting pedicab and told the driver to return to the tourist district. Flashing American quarters, he rounded up a half dozen shoe-shine boys and paid them to scour the streets for Helene. He contacted an old Syrian paperman, the only source of forged passports in Vanduu, and begged him to call if Helene showed up. He left word with every zonked-out ex-pat living on a boat, with every drug smuggler he'd ever done a favor for. He even asked his karaoke girlfriends to keep their seashell-pink ears cocked, their thickly mascaraed eyes open.

Then he waited. For over forty-eight hours. In the hotel where Helene had once stayed. He thought that maybe she'd come back. He knew she must be terrified, trapped in the capital, most likely within ten square blocks of him. The police were canvassing the bus depot day and night. The border crossing to Minaphor was heavily guarded. Vanduu had no airport. The only functioning ferry landed in his village on Mondays and Fridays, which was why, on day three, Finster went home.

He climbed off his hammock, nudged his dogs out the door, then headed toward the pier. The ferry was just visible on the horizon, its decrepit prow carving a wedge of foam through the glassy swells. In Vanduuan lore, a boat tugs a whole new ocean behind it. Ocean eats ocean. New world devours old. The foam is the mark of its voracious appetite. Teeth of the dog, the natives call it.

Flanking the wharf's narrow entrance, the hawkers had set up their slapdash bazaar. Finster hurried through it, ducking under tarps, then hopped up onto the pier and squinted into the distance. Another perfume shipment was coming in, but he couldn't have cared less. He leaned against a piling and waited. When the ferry finally chugged up to the dock, he watched, with a gloomy pang of déjà vu, as the passengers funneled out. When his shipment was hoisted out and chucked onto the pier, he didn't even check to see how many vials were broken. When his wild-haired carriers showed up joking and jostling, he shooed them away with uncharacteristic vehemence. The ferry was leaving again in fifteen minutes, shipping off to Jayapura, then Palau and the Philippines. It was probably Helene's only way off Vanduu, and he hoped, by some untenable miracle, that she'd know it. He prayed, with all the poignant, cross-your-fingers, stubborn, unconditional yearning of the besotted, that she'd appear.

A bowlegged boy helped his plump Papuan mother on board, followed by an Indonesian businessman chatting on a cell phone, six Filipina girls, two buzz-cut Vanduuan missionaries, and a meaty Palauan with three pink piglets in a bamboo cage.

A whistle, no louder than a teakettle, shrilled, and the gangplank was hauled up. Finster reeled around, scanning the wharf for any hint of Helene, but all he could see were the dejected hawkers behind their unsold trinkets and two policemen he hadn't noticed before.

He turned back to the boat. A spew of exhaust the color of tinsel and rust filled the air, and the ferry droned off.

A jolt of panic and hope overtook him; on the one hand, Helene was still trapped in Vanduu, but on the other hand, Helene was still in Vanduu. Shielding his eyes from the unrelenting sun, Finster watched as the ferry disappeared into the slosh and glare, until all he could see of it were teeth marks of foam.

The clack and clatter of the mah-jongg tiles sounded like a thousand teeth chattering, or the harbinger of a coming geological upheaval, or the brittle bones, within the channels of Helene's ears, being rattled to insensibility. For two nights, all night, she listened. But she did not dare ask the Chinese proprietor for another room. She didn't even allow herself to step into the hall at night. She bought her drinking water from the boy who swept the floors. She bought her cigarettes and liquor from the sixteen-year-old Filipina "hostitute" who lived next door. Her quarters, an eight-by-ten, tar-papered room behind a gambling parlor, had become a noisy haven, a smoky sanctuary, a dark theater in which she could replay, in mind-boggling detail, the scenes from last Monday. If the future snuck in, if she tried to fathom how she'd eat tomorrow, sleep tonight, get out of Vanduu, a weariness, as quick and kind as ether, anesthetized her.

She lay back on the sheetless mattress and lit a fresh cigarette with the smoldering stub of her last one. She watched the smoke spike out around her. Since she had no tangible evidence of Thomas's death—no weepy hospital scene, no stoic surgeon in green, no body, no funeral—it took everything in her being to accept the abysmal fact, and she needed to accept it, and all its ramifications, if she was to survive. In order to make it real, in order to make death visceral, she played the few scant memories she did have over and over again.

In the first one, she was back at the bar in the capital's main terminal, waiting for a bus to Mr. Khan's village. The instant Thomas had driven off, she knew she'd made a horrible mistake and had caught the first bus out of Baguay. She ordered a scotch and soda from the Filipino bartender and was about to down it, when, on the box-shouldered TV above his greased pompadour, she saw her passport photo. It filled the screen. The photograph had been taken years before, on the day of a ravaging migraine, and the effect of seeing her younger self—crimped, wan, and exasperated—on a black-and-white TV set in Vanduu lent it an especially hallucinatory cast. A newscaster, in Peter Sellers's absurd Indian accent, announced that two American tourists, Thomas and Helene Strauss, had struck a Muslim child with their rental car today, attempted to flee the scene, and while being pursued, Mr. Strauss had had a heart attack. Both he and the child were dead. Mem Strauss, last seen in the vicinity of Kampung Jaya, the child's home, was still at large.

The story was so ludicrous that Helene shook her head and laughed—snorted really—then turned to the man beside her and asked, "Did you hear what I heard?" The man was Indonesian and did not speak English. Or he pretended not to. But he recognized her. She could see that. The man looked frightened.

She had enough presence of mind to pay for her drink, which she immediately downed, before heading back into the terminal to look for another American, or an Australian, or someone culturally familiar. She wanted them to return with her to the bar, listen to the newscast, then tell her what they heard. But she was the only Occidental in sight. And she was noticeable. She hurried back to the bar, but she didn't go inside. She remained in the doorway, within the folds of the garnet-red drapery, and listened to the TV again, to the same absurd story—except now, the dead girl's picture was on the screen and it didn't sound absurd. It sounded terrifying. The bartender with his greased pompadour and glassy-eyed customers on one side, and the terminal with its smoking buses, screaming vendors, and surging crowds on the other, all seemed to be moving behind wax paper. She spied a policeman and started toward him when a tug of self-preservation pulled her back.

She took a measured breath and tried to focus. A young Chinese woman, dressed like a catalog model for Esprit, sat on a bench reading *Cosmopolitan*. Helene hunkered down beside her and said, "I think my husband is dead."

She said it not so much to elicit a response as to hear the words spoken aloud.

The Chinese woman got up and left. Helene turned to the next person on the bench, a Vanduuan woman in a flowing Mother Hubbard, and said, "My husband is dead." She also told the Indian woman on the next bench over. But no matter how many times she said it or whom she said it to, it rang with false sentimental cadences. To quell that, she assumed an offhanded tone, as if her husband had died years as opposed to hours ago, but an anguished pitch in the timbre of her voice caused her to break before she spoke. She walked up to complete strangers, opened her mouth, but nothing came out. Then she started to sob, but she maintained just enough presence of mind not to weep in full view of the terminal, not to be *that* conspicuous. She hurried over to the hawkers' stalls, to the din and bustle, and wept in secret, wept with the checked restraint of someone who cries during a ridiculously maudlin movie.

Finally, in order to stop crying, she took on the pose of someone who has been greatly inconvenienced by death, as if death were no more than a mixed-up hotel reservation, and told the trishaw driver who laboriously pedaled her through traffic to the hotel district, "It really doesn't matter how fast you go. My husband's already dead." Told the hotel clerk who refused her a room when she wouldn't give her name or show her passport, "I would have taken a single. I'm alone after all."

And this whiny, exasperated tone seemed to be the only possible way she could go on.

That was the first hour.

The next memory was of the night itself, the interminable hours after deadening shock had set in. Helene found herself sharing the doorway of an abandoned building with a Vanduuan woman and her two children, a remarkably silent baby and a boy with a skin disease.

The stoop was obviously the family's home. Two cardboard pallets had been laid out on the wide steps and a little black cooking pot on little black spider legs squatted over a blue Sterno flame.

"There's no other place for me to go," Helene explained, wedging herself in beside them. "The hotels won't let me check in because I don't have a passport." She could see the woman wasn't really interested in her explanation.

The boy lay down. His ears and neck looked as if they'd been thickly swabbed with calamine lotion until Helene realized that was the actual texture of his skin.

Neither she nor the woman closed their eyes.

"I won't sit on your cardboard," Helene assured her. And she drew her elbows in, her legs up, and tried to make herself as infinitesimal as possible. "Just pretend I'm not here."

But a couple of minutes later, she wrapped her arms around her knees and started rocking, slowly at first, then in deeper and more frenetic lurches. She could sense she was frightening the woman—she certainly was frightening herself—but she couldn't stop. It felt as if the balance of her being could only be maintained by rocking. She pressed the heels of her hands against her eyes, pressed them so hard that she actually saw a firmament of crumpled stars, and a surge of grief, so all-encompassing that it seemed to be like gas filling hollow space, finally brought her down and stilled her.

She tilted her head back against the filthy wall and tried to make sense of what happened. That Thomas had suffered a heart attack seemed inconceivable. More than inconceivable, *ludicrous.* Thomas's heart was perfectly fine; the man had cancer. And that he'd struck a child and tried to run away was beyond the realm of believability. For a moment, a jolt of hope revived her, because, if these facts were so blatantly wrong, the police might have mistaken someone else for Thomas. But then she remembered her passport picture on the TV, and once again, in stuporous shock, tried to jerry-rig a semblance of sense.

An eight-legged insect the size and shape of a nail clip started up her leg, and she watched it with benumbed fascination.

Where was she when it happened? Probably still at the Chalets. Probably brushing her hair. *I was brushing my hair when my husband dropped dead of a heart attack after killing a child.* She could picture her plastic hairbrush, with her loose red hairs caught in its stubby bristles, with more clarity than she could envision Thomas's face.

She pressed her fist against her mouth to mute her sobbing. I can't stay here tonight, she thought, I should try to find help. And the concreteness of that idea, *that she should try to find help,* calmed her momentarily. It had all the outward appearance of a plan. But she didn't get up, she didn't even shift her weight. Instead, she squinted down the alley in both directions. In both directions, the night was the color of motor oil. The Sterno flame was still burning under the black pot, suffusing the doorway in waffling blues, and it occurred to her that the family used it as a porch light. The woman was slumped forward, snoring raggedly, practically squashing the baby. The boy was sprawled against her bare thigh, his eyes trundling back and forth under his scabby lids. *I told Thomas to pull over if he felt sleepy. I distinctly told him to pull over if he felt sleepy.* And the inevitable sequitur, without a jot of mercy, stepped forward. *I never should have let him go off alone. If I'd been with him . . .* But she stopped herself from going there. She couldn't go there. If she went there, she might not come back. So she retreated to the more palpable *I told him to pull over if he felt sleepy.*

If she tried to venture any further, if she tried to envision the moment that Thomas's heart gave out, her mind simply emptied out, like a bathtub.

Finally, like something unctuous leaking in from behind a wall, fatigue soaked through, and she let her head sink onto her knees. She couldn't tell if she was actually sleeping, but at least she wasn't thinking. When she opened her eyes again, a bar of white sunlight was crossing her legs (a line of brightness, which in the momentary delay before full consciousness appeared to be a dazzling ray of compassion). She abruptly sat up, then remembered exactly what she was doing here.

The woman and the boy were still asleep, curled on their cardboard pallets. The baby lay face up on a blanket beside them, a piece of mosquito netting draped over him, like cheesecloth draped over a game hen. Helene knew she shouldn't wake them. Why would they want to wake up especially early to face another day of this? But she could hardly just sit there and wait for them to get up on their own, so she nudged the woman's shoulder.

"I'm sorry to wake you," she said, "but it's an emergency."

The woman blinked sluggishly at Helene, then sat up and let her gaze drift to a vague space beside Helene. She wore no discernible expression whatsoever, at least none that Helene could read.

"Please," Helene said. "I need your help. I can pay." She dug into her purse and hauled out a fist full of coins. She held them out to the woman, having no idea how much they were worth.

The woman studied the coins, then woke her son.

"I need to get to the American embassy," Helene explained, thinking, Surely, someone at the embassy will know how to help. They'll know where Thomas's body is. If she could just see his body, everything would, if not exactly make sense, at least become real. "Do you know where it is?"

The woman was still staring at the coins.

"Does he?" Helene asked, pointing to the boy.

Neither seemed to know, or, at least, neither changed their expression. Helene stood up. Her legs felt like blocks of balsa wood. Another family was sleeping across the way. "Would they know?"

When the woman saw where Helene was looking, her whole demeanor went through quick transformations. She scrambled to her feet and took hold of Helene's wrist, then yanked her son to his feet and said something to him in Vanduuan. Helene could see the woman had no intention of sharing her new patroness with the family across the way.

She turned her full attention back on Helene's coins, plucking from Helene's cupped hand whatever amount she seemed to deem fair, then gestured for Helene to follow the boy. He was already loping down the alley. Even in the tender light of morning, Helene could see that the soles of his feet held the same waxy ridges as his neck.

She hurried after him. He was heading into some sort of no-man's-land—a swath of abandoned warehouses between the tourist district and the tin-and-tarp suburbs. Now and again, children would emerge from boarded-up doorways, holding out cellophaned Chiclets or single, water-stained cigarettes for Helene's perusal, but she ignored them. A cow with teeth as big as piano keys stood in the middle of the road. The boy hardly seemed to be leading her toward embassy row.

She caught up with him and grabbed the hem of his T-shirt, yanking him to a standstill. "Do you speak English? This can't possibly be the way to the embassy."

"Telefon."

"You're taking me to a telephone?"

The boy nodded.

She glanced around, trying to imagine what a phone would be doing here.

"Is it much further?" she asked.

He shook his head no, then gestured up the street. He didn't exactly point. He didn't exactly do anything as reassuring as point. He simply crumpled his fingers loosely and flapped his wrist, as if he was throwing rice.

She finally let go of his T-shirt and hurried after him, sticking close, practically trodding on his shadow.

When the warehouses finally gave out—crumbled from shell to wall to rubble—she found herself in a neighborhood of identical plywood shacks, with identical electric-blue tarp roofs. The shacks were on little cul-de-sacs, arranged around a drainage ditch, like suburban tract houses are arranged around an artificial lake.

An ancient rotary pay phone was bolted to a pole. When Helene walked up to it, she saw that the instructions were in Hindi. She picked up the receiver. The instrument was scalding, the mouthpiece square, the numbers as indecipherable as glyphs. For a moment, the task of tackling this alien object with a purse full of nonsensical coins, only to confirm that Thomas was dead, seemed beyond doing.

The boy was shambling away, eyeing a vendor's blanket. As far as Helene could see, the blanket was piled with chintz and dregs. "Don't leave!" she told the boy. "I need your help."

She scooped another handful of change out of her purse. "I don't know which coins to use."

The boy gingerly plucked out three, then handed them to Helene. She threw them into the slot and dialed the operator.

"Do you speak English?"

"Yes."

"I need you to put me through to the American embassy."

"Yes. No problem. One minute."

The vendor was struggling to his feet, extending an arm toward Helene. She was terrified that he recognized her, that he was pointing her out. Bangles dangled from his forearm, and it took her a second to realize that he simply wanted her to buy one. She waved him away.

The operator came back on. "Sorry. No embassy."

"What do you mean there's no embassy?" Helene said. "There has to be an embassy. Please, it's an emergency. Could you try again?"

"Yes. No problem. One minute . . . Sorry, no embassy."

"I don't understand. Do you mean there's no embassy or you can't get through?"

"No embassy."

"That's not possible," Helene said. "Is there a consulate?"

"Yes. No problem. One minute."

Helene heard a click, a crackling void, ethereal gibberish, then the familiar drone and pulse of a ringing phone.

"U.S. consulate." The receptionist had the adenoidal accent of an American.

"I'm a U.S. citizen," Helene said. "I need help." She tried to blot out the tumult and push of Vanduu. The vendor, undaunted, was now holding up the array of his wares—pencils, batteries, fly-ridden sweets, a towel replete with palm trees that spelled Vanduu.

"One moment. I'll transfer you."

A violin rendition of "We Are the World" came on, and its vaulted crescendo, all strings and sap, seemed to be, in that hallucinatory moment, the essence of America.

"Yes?" a man answered.

"I'm an American citizen. My husband just died. I need your help. *Please.*" Her voice, to her own ears at least, sounded teeny, whizzing, atonal, like a squeak coming out of a plastic doll.

"Mrs. Strauss?"

"How do you know my name?"

"We've been expecting your call."

She shut her eyes and started rocking on her sandaled feet, mashing the palm of her free hand against her lids. "Oh, thank God," she said. "Do you know what happened to my husband?"

"As far as we know, he died of a heart attack around eleven A.M. yesterday. You have our condolences."

She let her hand slide over her mouth and started sobbing. "Then it's really true?"

"We're very sorry for your loss, Mrs. Strauss."

"I want to see his body."

She heard a muffled voice, the bark of an answer, and her own piping breath breaking against the receiver.

"We can make that a condition. That's a can-do. Would you like to come in, Mrs. Strauss?"

"I don't know where you are. I don't know where I am. Can't somebody come get me?"

"Give me a moment." She could hear him talking to someone else. "That's a can-do. But we need to know where you are. We need your help. Can you see any landmarks?"

She could only see tin, tarps, and plywood, and the vendor, who was now holding up a pair of ceramic hula girls. With desultory posturing, he tried to demonstrate how they could be used as salt and pepper shakers.

"I'm near some abandoned warehouses, in some sort of plywood suburb. It's not that far from the hotel district. Will you take me to see Thomas's body?"

"As I said, we can make viewing your husband's body a condition. Listen to me, Mrs. Strauss, can you ask someone where you are?"

"A condition of what?"

"Ask one of the passersby where you are."

"A condition of what?"

"Your husband's body is under Vanduuan jurisdiction. I'm afraid it's not up to us. It's up to the Vanduuans. We can make seeing your husband a condition of your coming in."

"Coming in *where?*" She suddenly didn't like the sound of "coming in." "Coming in" did not sound promising. "Coming in" sounded like a stock phrase spoken by the control tower to a hysterical stewardess in a B movie after the jumbo jet's pilot and copilot have had heart attacks, or been shot by terrorists, or contracted micro-plagues that have rendered them blind.

"We can escort you to the police station, Mrs. Strauss. We can maintain an OSP, an on-sight presence, to make sure that the Vanduuans treat you according to international law. We can provide you with a list of excellent Vanduuan lawyers, all of whom speak English, all of whom we'll vouch for."

"I don't want a lawyer. I don't need a lawyer. I'm not going to any police station. I'm going to collect my husband's body and go home."

"That's not something we can help you with, Mrs. Strauss."

"You can't talk to the Vanduuans, for God's sake? You must be able to negotiate."

"We have no jurisdiction. You're under Vanduuan law, Mrs. Strauss."

"Can't you give me asylum?"

"We don't maintain a physical mission. We have a presence, a consulate, Mrs. Strauss."

"Why do you keep saying my name all the time? Is someone else listening in?"

"Trust me, Mrs. Strauss, the Vanduuans haven't exactly mastered phone tapping. The Vanduuans haven't exactly mastered the push-button phone."

"I want to speak to whoever's in charge. I want to speak to the ambassador."

"This isn't an embassy. We don't have an ambassador."

"Then let me speak to the consulate."

"At present we have no consulate."

"Who the hell are you?"

"I'm the economic attaché."

"I know someone else is there. I can hear you talking to someone."

"Mrs. Strauss, calm down, please. We all want the same thing. We want your safety. We want incident prevention, not incident control, do we not? If you'll just listen to me, we can bring you in safely."

She began rocking again. Whatever he was saying fractured into white noise. "I can't think," she said.

"Let us think for you, Mrs. Strauss."

That terrified her.

"I've got to go now," she said. "I'll call back later."

"That's not advisable, Mrs. Strauss. You don't want the Vanduuans to pick you up without our being—"

She hung up. She lightly rubbed her lips and cheek, as if they were insentient, anesthetized. The boy was squatting in a wand of shade thrown by the telephone pole.

"Don't go anywhere," she told him.

The street had become jam-packed. Families as big as herds were funneling out of their tarp doors, dragging knots of laundry and tin cooking pots out onto the cement curbs.

Helene stared at the crowds and tried to figure out what to do next. She couldn't stay here, not in full view of the street, but she didn't want to give up the telephone. The telephone was crucial. She couldn't think clearly, but she knew the telephone was crucial.

"I'm going to make another call," she told the boy. Rifling through her purse, she grabbed more coins and jammed whichever ones would fit into the slot. She rotated the ancient dial back to operator.

"I need to place a collect call to the United States." She wasn't quite sure who she'd call first, but she'd call someone. Thomas knew important people, men who worked in the State Department, who obtained papers for him to travel to countries with bullet-riddled borders, who had visa extensions delivered to him in remote Amazon villages as promptly as pizza is delivered in the suburbs. Surely, men like that could overrule that horrid flunky at the consulate.

"Maaf. Vitcom."

"Do you speak English? I need to talk to an operator who speaks English."

"Yes," the same voice said. "May I help you?"

"I need to make an international call, *collect*."

"Sorry. Must to place at Vitcom terminal."

"Vitcom? I don't know what that means. It's an emergency. Please, I have a calling card. I just can't punch it in because I'm at a rotary phone. Can you do that for me?"

"Sorry. Vitcom."

"I don't know what the fuck Vitcom means." She turned to the boy. "Do you know what Vitcom means? Do you know where there's a terminal?"

He nodded.

"Is it far?"

He shook his head.

"Thanks for nothing," Helene told the operator, and hung up.

They started off again, skirting the perimeter of the plywood subdivision. Whenever they passed a vendor's stand, or a family selling something—and everything was for sale, the tin pots, the rags that doubled as laundry, the rows of ugly, garish batiks that someone must have cooked up in a cauldron—both men and women surreptitiously eyed her. Children dogged her. Not aggressively—after all, these were the families who didn't have the means or savvy to secure even a slab of cardboard on a square of sidewalk in the tourist district. On one corner, a woman suddenly reached up and touched the hem of Helene's tank top. Helene almost screamed and bolted. It took her a moment to step out from the whirligig of her shock and grief to realize that the reason the woman was grabbing her had nothing to do with the death of a child in a distant kampung. A child's life span around here couldn't be much longer than a fruit fly's. No, the reason the woman had globbed on to her was that, even in her filthy tank top and disfiguring sorrow, Helene was the most promising thing in sight, the sole source of potential income for as far as the eye could see.

The boy veered into an alley, zigzagging around tin fences, a demolished churchyard, a silted-up sewer, a tiny shrine tiered like a wedding cake. When they finally emerged back onto the fuming streets, they were in Chinatown.

The vendors here did not sit passively. They held up their electronic gizmos and bleeping alarm clocks, and shrieked.

Across eight lanes of traffic, Helene could see a barred glass storefront draped with a shredded plastic sign that read: VITCOM VANDUU'S INTERNATIONAL TELECOMMUNICATIONS: JOIN THE TWENTY-FIRST CENTURY AND BE IN TOUCH WITH THE WORLD!!!!

Two uniformed teenagers, each sporting a sea-green helmet and a machine gun, stood posted beside the gated door.

"Who are they?" Helene asked. "Are they police?"

The boy shrugged.

"Soldiers? Private guards?"

The boy didn't seem to know.

"Do they work for Vitcom or the government?"

The boy simply stared down at his scabby feet.

Helene stepped back into the alley. Someone had shoehorned a tar-paper shack between two buildings, and she leaned against it, letting her head topple forward. She grabbed hold of sunburnt knees and braced the weight of her being on them. A narcotized calm, the serenity on the far side of hysteria, finally stilled her. She sank down into a half-squat. She closed her eyes. All that she felt was exhaustion.

"Is there another Vitcom nearby?" she asked at length.

When the boy didn't answer her, she actually felt relieved. She doubted she had the wherewithal to stand up, let alone trudge another surreptitious route that led to another gated storefront, only to find more teenage police, or uncomprehending operators, or foreign phones with wires that, in the noonday heat, stretched like salt-water taffy.

Helene said, "I need to lie down. I think I might pass out."

The boy squatted beside her.

"Not here!" she said. She ran her hand over the back of her neck. Her hair felt gummy, her skin dusted with grit. She unsnapped her purse and dug out a coin. She had no idea if she was handing the boy a half-penny or a mini-fortune. "You have to help me. I have to lie down. I'm not feeling well. Do you know someplace where I can lie down for a while? And I'm not going back to your mother's stoop, so don't even think about it."

She scrutinized the child while he studied his coin; there was always the possibility that he barely spoke English and had no idea what she was asking.

"Can you take me to a hotel? Someplace they won't care about passports?"

"Peng-X?" the boy said.

"Fine. Take me to Peng-X's."

The boy rose to his feet and started trotting down the alley.

"Slow down!" Helene shouted, trudging after him. "I can't keep up with you."

But it wasn't really true. At the thought of losing sight of the boy, a new, mounting panic infused her with boundless energy. She almost overtook him, treading on his bare heels.

When they passed the demolished churchyard again, Helene noticed that the cinder-block chapel was mostly intact. Over the incessant din of the city, she thought she heard faint singing coming from within, and a vague memory materialized, spliced together from the Hollywood films of her girlhood, of a young, handsome European priest leading his native parishioners in beatific hymns.

She suddenly had the mad idea that there *was* a priest inside who would take her in and give her asylum.

She told the boy to wait in the alley, then hurried through the courtyard, stepping over pieces of rubble the size of popcorn. The singing grew louder, but it no longer sounded beatific, it sounded frenzied. When she finally reached the chapel's doorless portal, all that she found were swarms of feral cats, with necks as thin and bald as empty toilet paper rolls, yowling.

She walked back across the crumbling courtyard. "Just take me to the hotel, for God's sake," she told the boy.

They continued down the alley, which only seemed to spawn more alleys, until they came to a tributary of alleys. Jutting out of a riot of tin roofs stood a wooden, humpbacked building, with a slapdash tar-paper wing attached. The boy balled a fist and made his rice-throwing gesture.

"That's the hotel?" Helene said.

The boy nodded.

A half dozen Chinese men were loitering out front. If they noticed Helene at all, and they had to have noticed her, they gave no indication. They were watching a Filipina girl filling up a plastic jug at the hotel's hand-pump. The girl wore a vinyl miniskirt tighter than an Ace bandage and a dirty white apron. She looked like a hybrid between a prostitute and a maid.

"Ask her to come over here," Helene told the boy.

The boy shouted something in Vanduuan, and the girl sashayed over. Her face, smudged and smeared with last night's makeup, still retained its baby fat.

"Do you work here?" Helene asked.

The girl nodded.

"Do you know if there's a room for rent? I just need to lie down for a couple of hours."

She indicated that Helene should follow her.

Helene reached into her purse and scooped out her change, an act not missed by the girl. She gave the boy another coin. "Don't move," she told him. "Stay right here. I may still need you."

Then she followed the girl through the back door into the tar-paper wing. The owner, an elderly Chinese man whose face was as intricately lined as a shattered windshield, didn't seem to care if Helene had a passport or not, as long as she paid cash in advance. He told the girl to show her to her room.

The rooms were confined to the tar-paper wing. The hallway was lacquered with old Chinese newspapers, and an occasional flyer from a strip show of thirty years ago. (The dancers, tiny-breasted Asian girls, all wore their hair in the style of the Supremes.) Sunlight eked in through chinks in the roof. Whenever Helene passed an opening to the cavernous main building, she saw dozens of Chinese men, each in their own bubble of smoke, hunched over mah-jongg tables. The din was ear-shattering.

The girl stopped outside a row of tin doors and pushed one open. The door had no lock. Its knob was a fat nail. Twenty-four hours ago Helene would have cringed at this hovel of a room, but now she looked gratefully around—mattress, light bulb, a door she could close. She ached to lie down.

But the girl didn't leave. Helene wondered if she was hankering for a tip. She reached into her purse and dug out another coin, but stopped short of handing it over. She clutched it in her fist, just above the girl's outstretched palm.

"Is there a phone in this hotel?" she asked. She couldn't imagine there'd be a phone, but then again, she couldn't imagine this was a hotel.

"No, no."

"There's no phone? The owner doesn't have a phone?"

"Portable."

"What does portable mean? You mean he has a *cellular phone?*"

The girl nodded.

"Do you think he'll let me use it?"

She shook her head no.

"I'll pay him. Will he let me use it if I pay him? Will you ask him for me?"

She adamantly shook her head no.

"I need to make an overseas call."

"Vitcom."

"Yes, yes, I know all about Vitcom."

Helene shut her eyes and tried to blot up her dripping, stinging lids with the heel of her hand. She could feel rivulets of sweat meandering down her back. She had to lie down, but she was frightened that if she did, she wouldn't be able to rest, and she *had* to get some rest. Without a hiatus from this nightmare, she didn't think she could go on. "Can you buy me some liquor?"

The girl smiled shyly. "Okay."

"Scotch? Whiskey? Anything, I don't care."

"Okay."

She let the coin topple into the girl's palm, then ladled more coins from her purse and told the girl to take what she needed for the liquor. The girl sifted through the coins with the same bated-breath scrutiny that one employs when trying to select a winning raffle ticket. Helene assumed the girl was cheating her, but she hardly cared.

As soon as the girl loped off, Helene shut the door, jammed the room's sole piece of furniture, an orange crate, against it for a modicum of privacy, then sat down on the edge of the mattress and sobbed. She couldn't tell if she was crying for Thomas or herself. When it finally dawned on her that the walls were tar-paper thin, and that everyone in the hotel could probably hear her, she made a feeble attempt to muffle her mouth with a cupped hand. She thought, I'm going to lose my mind, they're going to find me in here without a mind. Then what can they do to me? What can they do to a madwoman? Let them be an On-Sight Presence to *that.* The very idea that the horrid man at the consulate had even suggested that letting her see Thomas's body be a condition . . . *a condition?* Thomas was dead. The condition *was* death. And the irrefutability of his being dead seemed new again. This truly terrified her—it wasn't sinking in. It had to sink in, because if it didn't sink in, she'd remain in this state, and she couldn't remain in this state. This state was insufferable. If she could just sleep for a while, she was sure it would sink in.

When the girl returned with the whiskey, Helene practically shoved her out the door, wedged the orange crate back into place, then opened the bottle and took a long gulp. I have to do something, she thought. As soon as she calmed down and slept a little, she would try to find another Vitcom, or go back to the tourist district and get someone to help her. Maybe they could make the phone calls for her? But she had no idea where the tourist district was. She had no idea where she was. She couldn't just wander around the city. She didn't exactly blend in. She had red hair, for Christ's sake. She could always get one of those Muslim get-ups. She opened her purse and poured out her money—four American twenties, one ten and two fives, and a dwindling puddle of Vanduuan coins. Instead of denominations stamped on their tin faces, the coins sported lizards, fruit bats, and bush pigs.

She started weeping again.

Why did he have to drive off alone? Why did she make him drive off alone? She should have gone with him to the village. And the thought of the village—the flyblown village—now seemed idyllic. She knew Finster lived there. She heard Mr. Khan say that at the caves. Suddenly she remembered Thomas and Finster beside her under dripping stalactites. Thomas's face was etched with distress. Could he have known that she'd slept with Finster? Her heart hollowed and crimped into a roaring nautilus.

Don't go there, she thought, don't even touch that. She took another stiff gulp.

She was sure she had enough money to hire a taxi to Finster's village—suddenly the idea of being whisked away in an air-conditioned taxi to someone who would take care of everything seemed so painfully good. Finster had to return to his village at some point. He'd surely help. The man claimed to be in love with her. He must know someone who knew someone important enough to help. And he had to have a phone. The man was probably a drug smuggler. Didn't they all have cellular phones? They certainly did in New York. And if Finster wasn't around, she'd go to Mr. Khan—it was his fault they'd come to Vanduu in the first place. Or she'd just attempt to sneak onto the ferry. She tried to remember if she'd seen any officials on the dock when they landed, but all she could remember was the staggering sun and the stench of rotting fish heads. She rubbed her eyes vehemently to stop crying. She looked down at her filthy feet, at the little strings of blood rubies where she must have scratched her ankles. Obviously, she thought, I can't be responsible for myself any longer.

She took another swig. I should put this into motion now. I should get up and do something now. But she didn't get up. She didn't move. She didn't even leave her bed. She continued knocking back gulps, because when she wasn't drinking, she had the nagging, inconsolable inkling that maybe, just maybe, she was responsible for Thomas's death.

She drank. Nonstop. And smoked incessantly, hoarding her meager matches by keeping a cigarette perpetually burning. She didn't, however, hoard her liquor. When one bottle ran out, she immediately bought another from the girl—scotch or gin or a Vanduuan brew with a proof higher than wood alcohol. When she wasn't drinking, she slept the parched, roiling, rubbery sleep of the soused. In those tenuous moments between unconsciousness and inebriation, when she wasn't dwelling on Thomas's death, she tried to rally herself to get up, to get help, but she could barely negotiate her way to the hotel's outhouse, let alone the Vanduuan streets.

She lost track of time: Her watch was missing, her room had no window. Sometimes, over the racket of the mah-jongg tiles, shouting matches erupted, or she could hear the sonorous, metered grunts of sex through the walls, but the noises that reached her seemed to come from other dimensions, vapor worlds. What astonished her was how quickly she'd adapted to this state, to this room—how workaday even horror had become. If she didn't contemplate the future, with its endless unfurling of grief, if she didn't obsess about the past, and her culpability in Thomas's death, she was able to maintain a modicum of—if not calm—nonexistence.

Sometime in the middle of the night (Helene wasn't sure which night), a man came into her room. He was shaped like an oil drum and wore the garb of a businessman: white polyester shirt, black polyester slacks. Even in her besotted state, she could see he was drunk, belligerently drunk. When he stumbled over the orange crate, he shouted Chinese obscenities with such shrill, slurred rapidity that he sounded like an auctioneer on helium.

Helene lay stock-still, realizing with sudden dread that she understood nothing—neither where she was, nor what she was doing there.

A veneer of terror, almost like a heat rash, covered her, but she still didn't move. There was an impossible decision that had to be made for either flight or inertia, self-preservation or willful obliteration, but she couldn't get herself to make it.

She watched in numb muteness as the man groped his way through the darkness toward her. He was muttering something, while simultaneously trying, with cloddish yanks, to undo his belt.

Then the door opened again, and Jing, the little "hostitute" who sold Helene her liquor, stepped in. In silhouette, she looked like a flamingo, all plumage and stilt legs. She caressed the man with a mockery of desire, stroking his polyester collar as one strokes silk. She rubbed up against him and giggled. She lay the tiny starfish of her hand against his voluminous white chest and gently admonished him for desiring another girl. With icy, efficient coyness, she slowly lured him out of Helene's room and shut the door.

For the first minute or so, Helene felt only stunned relief. She automatically reached for a cigarette and a drink, but her fingers wouldn't close around the cigarette. When she looked down at her hand, she could see it wasn't just cramped, it was shaking uncontrollably, and this physical manifestation of terror opened the way for a whole slew of terrors—the barrel-shaped drunk, the unlockable door, the tar-paper room, the violent shouts from the gambling parlor, the fact that she hadn't the slightest idea what she was doing. And there were other fears waiting in abeyance to come forward—

the whole incomprehensible future without Thomas. And she was only in the antechamber of fear, because in the main room, how she would get out of Vanduu awaited her.

She clamped her hands between her thighs to stop herself from shaking. Had she had a jot of will, a hint of direction, she would have bolted then and there.

Instead, she crawled over to the door and sat with her full weight pressed against it. As much as she craved a cigarette, she was too frightened to leave her post to fetch one. A half-empty bottle of gin was within easy reach and she quickly polished it off.

When she woke up, the air was already sweltering. It must have been mid-morning. She cracked open her door to check that the hallway was empty, then padded across it and knocked on Jing's door.

"*Vila masuk,*" piped a tiny voice.

Helene sighed impatiently. "I forgot what that means."

Jing opened the door, smiling shyly. Clumps of her bangs were twisted and sheathed in silver foil. "Come in. It mean 'Please come in.'"

The room had the same floor plan as Helene's—an eight-by-ten tar-paper cell. Three Filipina girls glanced up at her from a mattress on the floor. Helmeted in curlers, they looked more like adolescents asprawl on a suburban bed than prostitutes. One of the girls had jammed tiny rags between her toes so that her freshly painted red toenails wouldn't smear. A head shot of Jesus in weeping profile hung on one wall, and a photo of Madonna, evidently torn out of a magazine, hung on the other. Madonna's face, blanched by the concert lights, was tilted heavenward in saccharine ecstasy.

"Would you like some tea? We are having a hair party," Jing explained. "Would you like your hair done?"

Helene looked at Jing in befuddled amazement. Evidently, last night's incident was so commonplace, the child didn't even bother to mention it.

"You have such nice hair," one of the girls said, rising on her haunches and touching the ends of Helene's filthy red hair. "May I do your hair?"

"Jing, I need to talk to you."

'Okay."

"Alone."

"Okay. You heard my good friend Helene, go wait in the hall," she told the others.

As soon as they were alone, Helene said, "I have a favor to ask you, Jing."

"Okay."

"A big favor."

Jing scrutinized Helene, all the while twisting a strand of her silver-foil bangs around her index finger. Helene couldn't tell whether the girl was wary or merely sizing her up.

"I need you to find me a taxi driver who can take me to Pan'uu."

"Pan'uu?"

"The village where the ferry lands."

"Okay."

"I also need you to buy me one of those Muslim get-ups."

"Hijab?"

"Yes, yes, a hijab. You know I have money, Jing. I can pay you."

"Okay." Jing took Helene's hand, squeezing it with tenacious delicacy. "Will you stay for the hair party and tea?"

Helene shook her head no and tried to extricate her hand, but Jing held fast. The girl's eyes were riveted to her, and Helene finally understood that an additional trade was being made—her presence at Jing's party, and whatever status that afforded Jing, for Jing's help.

"All right," Helene said, "but just for a few minutes. Then I need you to find me that taxi and a hijab."

Jing finally released the hand and called the girls back inside. "My good friend Helene will stay for my party."

She motioned to the mattress, indicating that Helene should sit down, and Helene obediently sat.

"May I wash your hair?" the girl with the red toenails asked.

Helene glanced at Jing, caught her half-dictatorial, half-pleading look, and said, "Fine, you may wash my hair."

"May I curl it?"

"No, you can't—" Helene stopped, then studied her coiffeurs one by one—the girl with garish toenails, the one with fuchsia-pink hair, the one pitted with acne, and tiny, autocratic Jing. "Can you girls dye it?"

To Jing's great disappointment, she had no hair dye, but the girl with pink hair slipped out and returned with four plastic jars that looked as if they were filled with children's finger paints.

She set them on Helene's lap. Punky Colour Gelles. Helene read her choices: Fuchsia Pink, Plum, Rubine, or Witching Hour Black.

"May I dye your hair pink?" the girl asked.

"Oh, I don't think so," Helene said. "Let's go for Witching Hour Black."

Jing and the girls led her through the back of the hotel into the sun-baked courtyard where the outhouses stood. The courtyard's fence was pocked with star-shaped holes, the size of spouts on pop-top cans. Helene couldn't tell whether they were bullet holes or not. A plastic bucket sat under a rusty spigot.

Jing turned the bucket over, transforming it into a stool, then set off a rush of water. Helene sat down, shut her eyes, and bent her head under the tepid onslaught.

She couldn't tell if just Jing or all four girls were washing her hair at once, but for the first time since Thomas's death, she grasped the most primal and urgent of her losses—the loss of being touched. The girls worked with exquisite delicacy, kneading her scalp, caressing her neck, gracing the pads of their fingertips along her temples, her hairline, the back of her ears until Helene broke down and wept. She could sense the girls watching her, scrutinizing her—she could feel it in their touch—but whether an American woman's breakdown was an unbroachable subject, or whether jags of tears were simply commonplace occurrences in this hotel, the girls went about their business without so much as a pause.

When the dye was finally rinsed out, staining the ground the color of crude oil, Helene quickly splashed water on her face to dilute her vulnerability.

She followed the girls back into Jing's room, where she sat mutely under their scrutiny. They debated nonstop about the various possibilities for her makeover, all the while pulling, parting, and combing her hair. She didn't try to stop them. She didn't have the strength. She let them do whatever they wanted. She reasoned it would only make a better disguise. But, in truth, she ached to be touched, stroked, held, and this was as close as she could get.

When the rollers came out and her hair was finally unfurled, teased, and bouffanted, Jing took out a tiny compact mirror and showed Helene what she looked like. Helene thought she looked like many things—a drag queen, Elvira, a beehived Long Island matron, a go-go girl on *Hullabaloo*—but the one thing she didn't look like was her passport photo.

That afternoon, as soon as the other girls left, Helene asked Jing to follow her back to her room.

"You haven't forgotten what I asked you?"

The girl shook her head no.

"And you really think you can find me a ride to Pan'uu?"

The girl absently nodded, all the while her gaze skipped and skimmed over the bare contents of Helene's room—the crumpled silk tank top on the mattress, the Velcro sandals on the floor, the canvas knapsack chucked in a corner.

"Don't say you can do it if you can't do it, Jing. I need to know for sure. Can you find me a driver who can take me to Pan'uu?"

The girl nodded again, then touched a strand of Helene's hair, an oil-black spit curl wound as tightly as a slinky. "I think you look pretty," she said.

Helene sat down on the mattress, covered her face with her hands, and started laughing, a little too shrilly, a tad too long. Finally she wiped her eyes with the heels of her hands. "Thank you, Jing," she said to the flummoxed child.

Then, turning her back on Jing, she bent over and groped under the mattress until she found her pocketbook. She yanked it out by its leather strap and started to unsnap it, then stopped to study the girl—barefoot, knuckle-thin, ridiculously coiffured, ridiculously young.

"Can I trust you, Jing?"

"Oo-oo."

"What do you mean, *'oy, oy'*?"

The girl shrugged.

"Does that mean yes, Jing?"

The girl nodded.

Helene plucked out a twenty-dollar bill, then held it up by both ends, as one holds a flash card up to a child. "Is this enough to buy a hijab?"

"Oo-oo."

"I'll give you twenty now, Jing, and ten more when you return with the hijab and somebody who will drive me to Pan'uu."

"Okay."

"Tell whoever will drive me to Pan'uu that I'll pay them fifty American dollars, but only after I arrive safely, only *after* I get to the village. Is that clear?"

"Oo-oo."

Helene folded the bill in half, then handed it to Jing.

"You have any questions, Jing?"

"May I have your address in America?"

Reaching for a cigarette, Helene scrutinized the girl again. She had no idea what Jing was up to. "When you come back with the hijab and a driver who can take me safely to the village, then you can have my address in America."

Jing turned—no, pirouetted around and started toward the door.

"Come back soon, Jing!"

"Oo-oo."

Twelve hours later, Jing still hadn't returned.

In her room, in the chink of floor space between the mattress and the tar-paper walls, Helene paced and smoked. What unhinged her most, what caused her to crack from a frustration that at times superseded her grief, was her own stupidity. It wasn't just that she'd naively handed a desperate girl a fast twenty and the girl had cleverly vanished, it was that at Jing's age, she would have done exactly the same thing.

She crushed out her cigarette, then chucked it atop a mound of butts the size of a small ottoman. To quell another bout of tears, she mashed her brow against the door, mashed it so hard that she could actually feel her skin crimp and crease into the shape of corrugated tin. She didn't want to die in this place.

She threw what she had into her knapsack, then retrieved her pocketbook from under the mattress and counted her money for the umpteenth time.

Her plan was just desperate enough for her to put stock in it: She'd start walking toward the tourist district and, with any luck, stumble upon a Vitcom without guards, or a taxi driver who would whisk her off to Pan'uu, or tourists who would hide her in their hotel room, before she stumbled into the police. If she could just get to a phone, a hotel phone, if she could get a line out of this wretched country . . .

Closing the door behind her, she padded past the gambling parlor into the dark courtyard. At the far end, a corner of the tin fence had been ripped back and dog-eared. She crawled through it.

She was in some sort of alleyway, or drainage ditch—she couldn't tell which. A glow, dull as a dashboard's, wavered to her left and she figured it had to be the tourist district.

She started hurrying toward it. When she came to the first major intersection, she tried to recollect a landmark, a billboard, a street name, anything to orient herself. Chinese ideograms were branded on signs, painted on walls, fizzing in neon. A hurly-burly of busses and bicycles whizzed by.

For three days she'd existed in virtual isolation and the stimuli froze her in her skin. She retreated into a side street and elbowed her way through a small, socked-together crowd. When she looked around for the glow again, it seemed to have swapped places, to emanate from a different horizon. Unable to read the signs, she tried to read the addresses, but the numbers were as arbitrary as dice throws. She vaguely remembered Thomas telling her that the Vanduuan Chinese established their addresses by luck as opposed to logic, and suddenly his absence almost immobilized her.

In the burnt-out shell of a building, vendors were frying noodles in vats of oil. The smell—a potpourri of french fries and rose water—overwhelmed her: She became ravenous. She approached one of the vendors and poured onto his greasy cart what was left of her coins. The man studied the coins, then slid them into his pocket. He ladled out a glut of noodles, spilled them onto a paper plate, and jabbed a pair of balsa-wood chopsticks into the coiled mass.

Helene devoured them, oblivious of the hot oil still sizzling on their frizzy loops. When she finished, she was still hungry, but all her coins were gone, and she was reluctant to break one of her precious American bills.

She continued walking, but now she was completely lost. The main boulevards began fizzling out, turning from asphalt to dirt, and the streets lost all semblance of geometry. More and more of the doorways held the cardboard bedroom sets of the poor.

She abruptly about-faced and tried retracing her steps, but every alley bred another alley—crooked, puddled, reeking, packed with people selling everything from used flip-flops to rotten durians.

She clutched her pocketbook and kept walking. At the next major street, a diesel-blackened mosaic of bumpers and bicycles, she spied two soldiers dressed in the same sea-green uniforms as the ones she remembered from in front of the Vitcom. She scanned the street, but there was no Vitcom in sight. These two were standing under a billboard that said AMWAY: FREE ENTERPRISE AMBASSADORS! One sported Ray•Bans despite the darkness; the other slouched against a building, strumming his machine gun as if it were an electric guitar.

For a moment, Helene was tempted to turn herself in, end it here and now, hand over her hungry, thirsty, filthy body and exhausted will to someone—*anyone*—who would take charge of it. But something about the Ray•Bans—even more than the machine gun—caused her to step backward. A whirligig of bicycles engulfed her and she started walking. As soon as the soldiers were out of sight, she started running. She knew it was stupid, even dangerous, but she couldn't stop herself. She ran until the air felt as thick and hot as swamp mud. Then she leaned against a building and tried to catch her breath. When she finally looked up again, she saw the bright blots and strokes of neon ideograms. She'd gone full circle. She was back in Chinatown.

She walked for a block or two, until she spied the gambling parlor. It looked weirdly familiar, creepily comforting. She slipped around back into the puddled alley. It was too dark to see anything, so she ran her fingertips along the corrugated fence until she felt the opening. She crawled through it, tearing her tank top on a jagged tin tooth, then crossed the courtyard and went into her room.

She lay down on the mattress and closed her eyes. She didn't cry. She simply drew up her knees, wrapped her arms around them, and shut down.

Helene awoke to a grating tap on her tin door, like a pigeon scuttling across an air conditioner. It must have been close to noon. The temperature in her room was not only oppressive, it was stupefying. She stood up and cupped her eye to one of the countless nail holes that riddled the door. Jing was standing in the hall, bangled in dime-store trinkets and wearing a pair of new blazing-white sneakers.

Helene swung open the door. "Where the hell have you—" She stopped, sighed, and reached for a cigarette. "Did you get the hijab?"

The girl nodded, then squatted down, opened a bag, and pulled out a billowing, long-sleeved, lavender-and-plum, flower-sprigged shroud with a matching headscarf. The scarf was the size of a tablecloth; the shroud looked as if it would drag on the ground.

Helene closed her eyes, took another measured breath. "And the ride, Jing? Did you find me a ride to Pan'uu?"

"Oo-oo."

"Thank God." She embraced the girl, who, to Helene's embarrassment, hugged her back with desperate intimacy.

"The ride, Jing, where's the ride?"

Jing made a spider dance with her hand, then jerked her head in the direction of the alley.

"Bring them here," Helene said.

Jing left and came back with a boy of eighteen, nineteen tops, decked out in a leather vest and cuffed, ankle-high jeans. His hair was shellacked back with pomade and sweat.

"This boyfriend's cousin, Jimmy Umat."

Helene couldn't tell if he was Vanduuan or not. His eyes, which dodged and eluded hers, had a blue cast and an Asian fold.

"So you're my ride to Pan'uu, Jimmy."

Jimmy touched Jing's elbow, a gesture more proprietary than it was tender.

"Jimmy say he take you on his motorcycle tomorrow morning," Jing interpreted. "He say he need—"

"Why can't he take me right now?"

"Jimmy say he has business tonight. He say he needs twenty dollars for gasoline now."

"Tell Mr. Umat that twenty dollars would buy him enough gasoline to drive a convoy of tanks to Pan'uu. I'll give him five now, the rest when we get there."

"But Jimmy say—"

"Forget it, Jing, he'll get his money *after* I get to Pan'uu. Wait here." She closed her door and slumped against it. She didn't dare turn on the light, sure Jimmy would case her room through the nail holes. She was irate that the boy wouldn't take her right now, nervous about having to ride on the back of his motorcycle in full view of every policeman, every soldier. Kneeling down, she fumbled under the mattress and dug out her purse. Then she smoked a cigarette, thinking she could reinforce her illusory power by making Jimmy wait. When she opened the door, Jimmy was smoking his own cigarette. He flicked it onto the floorboards.

"I want you here first thing tomorrow morning."

Jing nodded.

"Is that clear, Jimmy?"

"Okay," Jing said.

"I want Jimmy to answer me."

Jimmy folded his arms (Helene could actually hear his leather vest creak) and nodded with exasperated annoyance.

Helene plucked a five out of her purse, folded it crisply in two, then held it out like a business card. "Deal, Jimmy? This is just a down payment. You'll get the rest *after* I arrive safely in Pan'uu."

Jimmy took the bill and crammed it into his watch pocket.

"Crack of dawn, Jimmy, in the alley and all gassed up."

"No problem," Jing said.

"I need to talk to Jing alone now."

Jing whispered in Jimmy's ear and he scuffed out through the gambling parlor. Helene watched as the white dog-bone shapes of his rubber zories flapped toward the blackjack table.

"Can I really trust him, Jing?"

"Oo-oo."

"Oy, oy is right. Come inside for a moment," Helene said, closing the door behind them. "Do you know how to wear the hijab, Jing?"

The girl shrugged. "I'm Catholic. Jesus Christ is my savior."

"Forget it."

"Jojo Muslim."

"The girl with pink hair?"

"Oo-oo."

"Can we get her to help?"

"She with customer." Jing said it as someone might say "She's with child."

"Never mind, I'll figure it out for myself." Helene opened the door again, but Jing wouldn't leave.

"You'll get the ten I promised you tomorrow morning, Jing, after Jimmy shows up."

"Okay." But the girl still didn't move.

"What now, Jing?"

"May I have your address in America?"

Helene sat down on the mattress and looked up at the girl, all cheap bangles and spider gestures. She couldn't imagine why Jing would want her address in America, unless Jimmy had concocted a scheme to wrangle more money out of her, and an address was the blackmail he needed. She scrambled through her purse for a pen and matchbook, then scribbled on the inside flap a slew of digits on a numbered avenue in Palooka, America.

In the dismal light, Jing read and reread the address, her lips moving as if she was committing it to memory. Then squatting down, she groped through her bag and pulled out an envelope.

"For you," she said, serving it to Helene on the platter of her open palms. "Open when you get to Pan'uu. Not minute sooner."

Then she slipped out the door. The envelope was handmade, scissored and glued together from a paper bag. Jing had scrawled in schoolgirl script on its piecemeal flap, *For Heline. Important!* For some mad reason, Helene suddenly believed that Jing was trying to warn her, or that the envelope contained a pass of some kind, a letter of introduction to an underground railroad of karaoke girls who would help her get out of Vanduu if things went awry.

Using the stem of her pen as a letter opener, she quickly ripped through the flap and pinched out the letter.

Deer Heline,

I have 8 brothers + 2 sisters in PI. I so lonelyness for missing my family. I don't want to go to abroad but for the poverty reason I forced myself to do it. Will you please be my pen pal? My hobbies are dancing and hair styling. I like Madonna + Tiffany + man who used to be Prince.

How about you, would tell me something about yourself + your family? We are Catholic. We believe in heaven and hell, and the teaching of Jesus Christ, our lord and savior. What religion are you? Can I visit you in America? Don't forget to write! Please be my pen pal! Remember me when you get back to America. I will be here with no one.

With great affection,
Jofelia P. Navarro

P.S Don't forget, my friend call me Jing!

Helene read the note with stunned compassion, then put it back into its handmade envelope, fully intending to do something for the child when and if she got home. She set the envelope down next to the head scarf where, despite good intentions, she forgot it the next morning.

Jimmy was over an hour late. As soon as Helene heard the motorcycle, she hitched up her ill-fitting shroud and squeezed through the dog-eared fence.

Swarms of Chinese were already emerging from their tin sweat boxes.

Jimmy sat astride a souped-up moped—lipstick-red gas tank, chrome exhaust.

"Where have you been?" Helene asked.

"You looked like you needed the extra sleep, *mem-sahib.*"

"For God's sake, let's just get out of here." Mounting the bike, she realized how hobbled she was in this cumbersome getup, how vulnerable. When Jimmy cranked on the gas and the bike lurched off, she was sure her hem would catch in the spokes, or her scarf, long as a wedding train, would snag around a passing pole.

She clung on to Jimmy's vest, to its studded leather belt. At stoplights, and in choked traffic, she kept her face averted. It was hardly necessary. They weren't even noticeable. Just one more leather-bedecked hoodlum and his fundamentalist moll.

When the city finally unraveled and the scrub jungle began, Helene allowed herself to experience a modicum of hope. She opened her mouth and let the wind dry out her being.

An hour later, Jimmy veered off the main road and came to a bumpy stop in a charred clearing. He killed the engine, then looked over his shoulder. "You pay now," he said.

Under the direct sun, without a breath of wind, the shroud immediately heated up like a flower-sprigged sauna. "I don't think so," Helene said.

"I think so," Jimmy said. "Pay now."

"Forget it, Jimmy. Our deal was Pan'uu. I'm not giving you a cent till we get there."

"Forget it, Helene. You pay now."

"You want me to pay now, Jimmy, I'll show you how I pay now."

She climbed off the bike, gathered up her hem, then strode across the burnt stubble to the main road. She planted herself in the middle of the yellow line, whipped off her head scarf, and began waving it like a football pennant.

"You see, Jimmy," she shouted, "I'm so goddamn hot in this asinine getup, I'm so tired of your shitty little island, I don't give a flying fuck if they catch me, I don't care if they shoot me. But before I die, I'm going to make sure they know it was Jimmy Umat who drove me here, Jimmy Umat who tried to help the dim-dim American murderer Imperialist whore escape."

Then she reeled around, faced the empty, heat-banded highway and screamed, "JIMMY UMAT!"

She turned to him again. "So you can take my money and dump me here, but you won't get far on your little put-put. I know, I've been all over this hellhole you call a country, and there's no place to hide. If it's the last thing I do, Jimmy, I'll make sure they get you, and when they do, I hope they string you up by your balls."

Jimmy was standing beside a whorl of ferns, half hidden in their hairy shadows. He climbed back onto his bike.

Helene sat down on the road, on the scorched asphalt. She would have wept, but she couldn't even muster up that much strength. A breeze kicked up, and she watched the head scarf blow away like smoke. She heard the sputter of an engine, but she couldn't tell if it was the moped, or a distant, unseen truck barreling down on her. She closed her eyes; she didn't care. When Jimmy finally pulled up beside her, she slowly rose to her sweaty feet, ambled over to the bushes, retrieved the gritty, dusty scarf, draped it over her Witching Hour Black hair, then mounted Jimmy's bike and took hold of his leather belt again.

They sped off as if nothing had happened.

Fifty-odd kilometers later, where the crushed coral road veered off to Pan'uu, Helene told Jimmy to pull over. The sign said 2 KILOMETERS and she decided to walk it. She didn't want to arouse the whole village with the roar of his moped. She took out her cash, carefully angling her purse so that Jimmy could peer into its mini-maw and see he'd gotten all there was.

While Jimmy straddled his bike and counted the cash, Helene stepped into the jungle. Her plan was to walk along the edge of the road, just this side of leafy coverage. But after a couple of yards, she couldn't bear it—the jungle's floor was gummy muck studded with limestone pinnacles.

When she finally heard the moped buzz off, she stepped back onto the road, veiling her face with the head scarf, though no one was in sight. She tramped over the coral shards, white and stinging as rock salt. There was no shade. She could actually feel the sun drilling through the scarf. After a couple more yards, she ripped off the scarf to catch a momentary waft of relief as the air graced her sweaty scalp. Then she peeled off the shroud, down to her sopping tank top. For a second, she could actually feel the pulse of a sluggish breeze on her skin. Then that, too, burned away. She knew she should put the shroud back on, but the thought of swaddling herself again in that hot tent was intolerable. She walked a little further. When she thought she spied someone coming up the road, a silhouette stippled in heat bands, all elongated shadow and burning matter, she stepped back into the foliage. Under the noon sun, every plant and rock steamed. The whole jungle hummed. The precariousness of her plan suddenly hit her: She had no money left, she had no idea where Finster lived, she didn't even know if he'd returned to Pan'uu. She trudged on, stepping over land crabs with pinchers the size of nutcrackers, until she came to the edge of the village. No one was around, nothing moved save for a parade of motley chickens. She sat down on a fallen palm to wait for darkness. She ached for a cigarette but she didn't have any left. She shut her eyes and hoped against hope that Finster was here. When she finally cooled down, she slipped the shroud back on, then draped her head in the scarf. If someone stumbled upon her, she could always pretend she was praying.

Finster's dogs were acting peculiar. Just as he'd find a comfortable position on his hammock, their flat, clammy noses would poke through, and they'd whimper to be let out. Soon as he let them out, he'd hear their scabby paws scratching to be let back in. So he propped the Quonset hut door open with a coconut, climbed back onto his hammock, set his Walkman on his stomach, lit a fat joint, and put on his earphones to wallow in peace and self-pity to *The Best of Leonard Cohen.*

He pressed rewind. He needed to start the cassette exactly at the beginning of "Suzanne," not one note less. In his mournful, jittery state, only "Suzanne" seemed to be able to calm him down.

On the floor beneath him lay the scattered shards of his hopeless search for Helene: a telegram from Parker that said "No new news," a stack of newspapers that told nothing, and two dozen phone numbers of false leads.

The tape whirred, clicked, then hissed forward:

Suzanne takes you down
To her place near the river . . .
And she feeds you tea and oranges
That come all the way from China.

He shut his eyes and envisioned himself standing near a river, not the sluggish, muddy estuaries of Vanduu, but a rushing river of quicksilver. He couldn't quite picture Helene—in truth, he could only conjure up a generic Helene, a silhouette of grace and sensuality, so he pictured a woman's hands, soft as the hands in a Palmolive commercial, holding between her flawless breasts a blood-red orange.

And she lets the river answer
That you've always been her lover . . .
For you've touched her perfect body
With your mind.

And he saw his mind, encased in his head, rubbing itself between those breasts, which made the most exquisite plopping sounds against his ears.

He took another deep drag and let the pot induce a stupor for the next cut, "Sisters of Mercy." In this tune, Helene was dressed in a black-and-white habit with nothing underneath, save for some shiny rosary beads hanging between her breasts. As his Day-Glo dreams coursed along with Leonard Cohen's pop poetry, one of his dogs started shaking his foot.

He tried to kick the dog away, but she wouldn't let go. Reluctantly, he opened his eyes.

A Muslim woman was silhouetted at the foot of his hammock. He reached over and lit the hurricane lamp, then shook his head in wonder and welcome.

"I need help, Finster," Helene said.

"My God, Helene? Are you all right?"

"Not really. Do you have a cigarette?"

"Where have you been? How did you find—?"

"You were smoking a joint on the beach—not too discreetly, I might add. I followed you here. May I have that cigarette now?"

"I don't smoke cigarettes."

"Damn," she said, yanking off the head scarf. He was astonished by her black hair. It didn't suit her one bit.

He slid off his hammock and fetched her a chair. He was desperate to touch her and feel if she was real. He ached to hold her. He knew only one way to that end, but he felt a tinge of guilt employing it. With genuine condolence and a trace of opportunism, he said, "I'm so sorry about Thomas. He was a really great guy."

He watched as her face, hard with resolve, stiff with stoicism, supported by the steely cords of her neck, collapsed, and her eyes brimmed with tears, and the rims turned rash red, and the skin took on the blotchy pink and blur of profound sorrow. It was a well of feeling he, himself, had never come close to. He found it breathtaking.

"Do you know what happened to him, Finster? I don't know anything."

"The newspapers said he had a heart attack."

"Do you believe them?"

Finster shrugged.

"Oh God, I don't even know where his body is." And she mashed her palms against her eyes and started sobbing.

He put his arms around her, cradling her head against his chest, cupping her shoulders which, in their rhythmic heaving, felt like a human heart beating in his hands.

He let her cry herself out. He had no handkerchief to offer her. She wiped her eyes with her sleeve, then dug into her pocketbook for the remnants of a tissue.

Squatting down before her, keeping his hand on her arm, on its faint dusting of down, lest her presence vanish in a puff of pot as so many other of his hallucinations had, he asked if she was hungry, if he could get her something to eat.

"I just want a cigarette, a bath, and someplace to sleep. I haven't slept in so long, Adam, I don't even remember what it's like."

The Quonset hut had no tub, but it did have an outdoor shower, a garden hose jerry-rigged to an iron cistern. He found her a fresh bar of soap and the cleanest towel he owned, then led her out back and set up the contraption—the flimsy, erratic spigot, the opaque plastic curtain.

He said he'd be right back with her cigarettes. But he didn't exactly rush off. He loitered behind some oil barrels and watched her. Once wet, the curtain turned as diaphanous as chiffon.

Helene stood stock-still for a moment, fully dressed, wasting precious rainwater. It made a racket at her feet. Then, as if flinging off burning clothes, she tore off the shroud, the tank top, the cutoffs, and plunged underneath, letting the water drill her.

Behind the blur of the curtain, she looked more like an apparition than flesh. Finster stared at the white shape of her, with its two clouds of hair, the jet-black on top, the russet below. The clash between the black and the red, between mockery and reality, disguise and sex, more than made up for his initial disappointment with her dye job. Under the sway of pot, he felt as if he was witnessing, in the disparity of color, in the crudeness of the dye and the vulnerability of the natural, the very essence of Helene, the core of her suffering and desires. He could barely tear himself away.

When he returned from the store with her cigarettes, she was waiting in the hut, wearing the shroud like a sarong.

"Sure I can't get you something to eat?" he asked.

She shook her head no, then fumbled with the cigarette pack, practically slicing open the cellophane with her thumbnail. Knocking out a smoke, she leaned into Finster's Zippo.

He noticed her hand was trembling.

She inhaled a couple of quick drafts. "Where can I sleep?" she asked.

"I keep a room in the village, next to Mr. Khan's."

"Not a good idea, Finster. I'll use the hammock."

"You can't sleep here, Helene, there's no mosquito netting."

"It's been a while since I've used mosquito netting. Don't worry about it."

"I'll stay with you. I'll sleep in the chair."

"No thanks, Adam."

She sat down again and drew up her knees. Smoke, convoluted as chaos, hung above her.

"Where have you been all this time, Helene? You can't imagine how I looked for you."

Reaching for another cigarette, she lit it with the burning stub of her last one, and puffed away. He could see she was on the brink of tears again.

"I'm exhausted, Finster. We'll talk tomorrow."

"You sure I shouldn't stay?"

"I'd prefer to be alone."

"I don't think it's a good idea."

"Please, Finster"—she gently touched his arm—"I'm too tired to argue."

He set his Zippo down next to her cigarettes, then rooted his hands in his pockets. "The door can be locked from the inside. I'll leave my dogs with you. They're good watchdogs."

"Thanks, Adam."

He closed the door behind him, then tapped on it.

"Helene, if the mosquitoes bother you, use my Walkman. At least you won't hear them buzzing. That's what I do." He suddenly remembered what was in the Walkman. "I'm afraid I only have *The Best of Leonard Cohen*."

"I prefer the mosquitoes. Good night, Finster."

He started off again, then spied a sleeping chicken. He grabbed it and returned to the hut, tapping on the door. "Open up, Helene."

His dogs whimpered as she unbolted the door.

He carried the squirming chicken inside, tossing it down. The creature flapped across the floor.

"Is this breakfast?"

"This is the jungle, Helene, you can't be too careful. Chickens peck at anything that crawls—tarantulas, centipedes, biting ants."

"Thank you, Finster."

She sighed, and he stepped back into the moonlight, walked a foot or two, then spun around. The door was shut, bolted. The Quonset hut, rusted and riddled with WWII bullet holes, leaked light, swirls of light, machine-gunned constellations, shrapnel suns. He waited until she blew out the hurricane lamp, until the last evidence of her presence vanished. Then he stared at the spot where the hut had just been—a black void against a black jungle. For a moment, he had the unnerving feeling that she wasn't there, that none of this had happened, that the whole conversation had taken place between him and smoke. It took everything in his being not to rush back and bang on the door.

Finster barely slept that night. In the room he rented at Auntie Blukuk's guest house, a two-story claptrap next to Mr. Khan's, he lay charged and reeling. Masturbation didn't help. Now that he'd actually held Helene in his arms, even if only to comfort her, masturbation felt as satisfying as chewing old gum. It seemed to Finster that he was psychically bound to her, that if she turned or tossed in her sleep, he felt the tug on his being. He awoke bleary-eyed, but with a sense of purpose he hadn't experienced in years.

He slipped on what he thought were his most flattering Hawaiian trunks, the fuchsia frangipani design, then brushed back his springy blond coils, roped them into a ponytail, combed his smear of a mustache, and brushed his teeth vigorously. He checked to make sure he had enough cash in his wallet and headed to the store. He bought everything he thought she might like, practically everything the little tin store offered—coffee, tea, orange soda pop, tinned biscuits, tinned crackers, tinned fish, chips, Spam, Japanese noodles, cigarettes galore.

He lugged the groceries down the mile-long stretch of beach to the Quonset hut. Setting them down by the door, he cupped his eye to one of the bullet holes and peered in. Helene was still asleep, curled up, her shroud bunched around her waist. He could just make out a slice of white thigh crosshatched by the stringy hammock. Finster kept his hammock slung low so that his dogs could jump on, and one of his girls had done so. She lay squashed against Helene, belly up, her hind leg draped over the edge. The other dog slept on the floor in a latticework of shadows. The sight of the three of them cut through his heart.

He slipped around back and unlocked the rear door. As quietly as possible, he laid out the tinned and packaged feast on a picnic table he used as a desk, then padded up to the hammock. He knew he shouldn't wake her, knew she needed all the sleep she could get, but he couldn't help himself. He grazed her shoulder with his fingertips. She bolted upright, stared at him, the dog, then sank back and closed her eyes. In the sprocketed sunlight, she looked gaunt, remote, exquisitely sad.

It took everything in his being not to touch her again. "Did you sleep well?"

She rubbed her eyes, blinked rapidly, took in the room with befuddled recognition. "Finster?"

He grinned. "Hungry?"

She shook her head no, then pushed the dog off and sat up.

"You sure? You have to eat, Helene."

"Thanks, Finster, but I'm not hungry." She swung her legs over the side of the hammock, then reached for the cigarettes. Clamping one between her teeth, she clicked the Zippo and took a long pull. "I need your help, Adam. I don't know who else to turn to." She exhaled, then immediately took another protracted drag. "Can you get me out of Vanduu? I really, *really* need to get out of here."

He knew that's what she'd ask, but up until this moment, he hadn't quite let it sink in. Last night, in the throes of stultifying sleeplessness, there was a part of him that hoped beyond reason that she'd want to stay, not for some indefinite period of time, of course—he wasn't an unreasonable man—but for as long as it took her to recuperate, say, a month.

"If I don't get off this island, Adam, it won't matter if they catch me, I'll have gone mad."

He wanted to help her. He could see she couldn't take much more. Even her smallest gestures—the way she snapped rather than turned her head, the way she clawed rather than scratched her mosquito bites—were frayed and off-kilter.

"I need to make some phone calls, some overseas calls. Can you get me to a phone, Adam?"

"I can try, Helene, but Vanduu's still in the Dark Ages. They've got this service called Vit—"

"I know all about Vitcom." She mashed out her half-finished cigarette and lit a fresh one. "You don't have a cell phone?"

He shook his head no.

"Can you find me one?"

"They're pretty rare around here."

"What about a fax? Can you send a fax for me? A telegram?"

"I'm afraid it would still have to go through Vitcom. Vitcom's owned by the government. I don't think it's safe."

"Listen, Finster, Thomas has a friend in the State Department, Jack McGuinnis. He's some big something or other. If we can just get a message to him, I'm sure he can help. At the very least, he can strong-arm those little shits at your consulate into helping." She used the palm of her cigarette hand to rub her eye vigorously. Finster watched as the burning tip swung precariously close to a wisp of her hair. "Do you know the consulate wanted me to turn myself in?"

"You spoke to the consulate?"

She nodded, then shook her head no. "I spoke to some flunky at the consulate. He offered me a peek at Thomas's body if I would turn myself in."

"Helene, I wouldn't count on anyone at the consulate. Even if Thomas's friend talks to them, they're not going to help. Trust me, they're the last people in the world who would help."

He dragged over a chair, hunkered down, and faced her. With an air of clinical solace, he sandwiched her shockingly thin hand between his and carefully explained that Vanduu was like a powder keg right now, that all the consulate cared about was placating the islanders long enough to procure a lease for a military base, that her fate was the last thing on their minds. She had to trust him; he got his information from a solid source. He assured her that he *did* have connections, important connections. He kept that part ambiguous, hoping that vagueness implied power. In his opinion, their best shot was to lie low for a while, then smuggle her out of Vanduu. All the other countries around here were fed up with Vanduu; no one would extradite her. Getting her out wasn't going to be easy; it would take time to figure out the safest route. Most important, he wouldn't let her take any unnecessary risks.

Nothing he said was untrue, but a roil of bile, a deep distaste for himself, seeped up. After all, he could have phoned one of his numerous smuggler friends, met them at an isolated airstrip, and had her flown out that afternoon. It would have been risky, but it would have been her risk to take.

He didn't mention that option. In his opinion, she wasn't capable of making the call. In his opinion, what she needed was rest, uninterrupted rest, and it only just happened to coincide with what he needed—*her.*

"I don't care what it takes, Finster. Do whatever you have to do. Just get me out of here. Please." She hoisted herself out of the sagging hammock and crossed the cement floor. She stood in the jamb of the rear door, squinting out at the sun. Locking her fingers behind her neck, she squeezed her elbows together, as if to clamp her head in a vise, then abruptly turned around. "I have no money. I don't know who you have to bribe or what it's going to cost, but I can't pay you back until I get home."

This wounded him greatly. "Helene, don't you know I'd do whatever it took for you?"

"Finster, I don't know anything anymore."

He got up and started to open a biscuit tin with a sardine can opener, when she asked, with perplexed irritation, what he was doing.

"Making you breakfast?"

"I don't want breakfast. I'm not hungry. I want you to do whatever you need to do, talk to whoever you need to talk to, arrange whatever you need to arrange. Please, Finster, just get me home."

This wasn't at all what he had in mind. What he had in mind was a morning of tender reacquaintance, with her turning to him for comfort and him providing it tenfold.

He tossed down the sardine can opener, rooted his hands in his pockets, and scuffed over to the rear door. "You haven't even told me where you've been, Helene. You can't imagine how I looked for you."

"Does it matter? I mean, really, does it matter?"

"It does to me," he said under his breath, and left.

He took the back route to town, along the goat path. From this angle, Pan'uu looked even more ramshackle than usual—piles of rotting coconuts, steaming goat turds, a rusted oil drum, the shredded remnants of a public announcement duct-taped to a water tank: DON'T START AN EXERCISE PROGRAM WITHOUT CONSULTING YOUR DOCTOR FIRST! A few tradespeople were already up and about—Mr. Idechong, the barber, Mrs. Enin, the chicken slaughterer and video store owner, and Mr. Khan, who knelt before the entry to Motel Paradise, pruning a bougainvillea with tentative snips.

Finster waved to him, and Mr. Khan, shifting his preoccupied gaze, waved back. He did not look good. His left eye was still swollen from the night the police had hauled him into their headquarters to grill him about his role in renting the two Americans the car. Only yesterday, when Finster had stumbled upon him standing alone in his coconut grove, next to his prayer rug, staring out at a resplendent sunset, he'd simply said, "This is not a world I'd have chosen to be born into."

At Auntie Blukuk's, Finster plodded up the steps, trying to unpuzzle what he was going to do next. He wanted to do right by Helene; he considered himself an honorable man. Crouched over his night table, map, pen, pad, and sweat blotter out, he tried to ruminate on her safest means of escape. But he couldn't concentrate. He kept picturing Helene, the impenetrable grief, the cold impatience. He could still feel the sting of this morning's rebuke. He wasn't exactly angry with her—the poor woman was obviously at her wit's end—but he was still hurt.

A freshly rolled joint sat on the bureau.

He tried to resist it, but it kept beckoning.

Three long puffs later, as he closed his eyes, a plan slowly unveiled itself. It was short on specifics about Helene's escape, but minutely detailed about how he might get her to love him.

This was Finster's plan, or at least the plan he proposed to Helene. She would leave by sea. In five days, a ferry bound for the Philippines was due at the wharf. The Philippines had no extradition with Vanduu; at loggerheads over fishing rights and tourist dollars, the two countries weren't speaking. Finster would accompany her all the way to Manila. Once they'd bribed their way past the local officials, they'd travel as husband and wife. It was infinitely safer, infinitely less conspicuous than traveling alone. They'd carry snorkles, fins, sunblock, tacky souvenirs, dog-eared *Lonely Planet Guides*, the whole footloose American tourist shebang. Meanwhile, Finster would arrange for her to have a false passport made. The rub was the photo. They'd have to use a Polaroid. They couldn't very well send her pictures out to be developed. Once they had that, though, he knew a Syrian forger in the capital who would take care of the rest. All Helene had to do was alter her looks a bit more—haircut, glasses. Nothing drastic. They only needed to clear the local boys, who hankered more for bribes than busts. Did she have any questions?

"You could be describing our escape from Alcatraz and it wouldn't seem any less bizarre."

"Just call me Clint Eastwood," he said, grinning foolishly. In truth, he felt ill. He hadn't the slightest idea if his plan would work. He wasn't even sure if the Syrian could do the job.

"Do you have a Polaroid?"

He held up an ancient Land camera with a flash the size of a klieg light.

"And a scissors?"

He produced a toenail scissors. "I'm afraid it's all I could find. Do you want to do the honors or should I?"

"Just cut, Finster."

He sat her down on a three-legged stool in the center of the hut and tentatively ran his pocket comb through her hair. He held the tangled clumps by the roots so as not to hurt her. When he could finally get his comb through the knots, he took a step backward, mopped the sweat from his eyes with the crook of his arm, and tried to figure out a style, a look, a coiffure that would suit her—anything less, a slipshod hacking job, might look suspect.

Helene folded her hands between her thighs and shut her eyes. With her hair combed flat against her skull, she looked smaller, more vunerable, and the oddest memory scuttled back to him—Mia Farrow, young again, sparrow-thin, married to an already decrepit Frank Sinatra, shocking the world by cutting off her *Peyton Place* locks and sporting a "Twiggy" cut. This was the ideal for which he aimed.

After a few snips, however, he intuited that Helene was crying. She didn't make a sound or shake, but he felt himself standing within an aura of sadness. When he finally clipped off the last strands, he asked if she was upset about the haircut.

She shot him a look of unabashed incredulity, as if the haircut was so utterly beside the point, so minuscule within the scope of things, that he felt like a fool for having asked.

He rummaged through a cardboard box, found a pair of horn-rimmed sunglasses, punched out the tinted lenses, and handed the frames to her. He also dug out an old white sheet and duct-taped it to a wall.

Without so much as grazing her wrist, he posed her in front of the sheet, placed the Clark Kent glasses on her nose, stepped back and squinted until he could envision the best angle, then picked up the camera and started snapping—and once again, he felt a suffusion of sadness, as if the popping flash were irradiating something beneath her visage, not quite skeletal, more like an armature on which grief was hung.

When they finally had enough photographs, he fetched a jug of bottled water, poured out two glasses, then sat down beside her and quietly explained that she couldn't remain here, in the Quonset hut, while they waited for the ferry. It was too close to the village. His customers might drop by. One mile south, in the next cove, was an old plywood fishing hut that he sometimes used when he needed to get away from it all.

"I thought we were away from it all. I thought this village was the ragged edge of the universe."

"You'd be surprised. Pan'uu can get stressful."

She lowered her head, and for a moment he thought she was crying again, but when she looked up, he saw she'd been laughing.

"I use it to write in," he said defensively. It was a lie, but he liked the sound of it. Besides, it was only a partial lie. When he'd first come to Vanduu, he'd had every intention of writing poetry, perhaps even a novel, capturing Vanduu in meter and rhyme, as Gauguin had immortalized Tahiti in paint.

Unfortunately, the only poetry he'd written of late had been seduction ditties to the karaoke girls. Actually, he hadn't even written those. He'd pilfered the lyrics of Leonard Cohen, altering a word here and there to give it a tropical spin, then pawned them off as his own. The girls, desperate to be loved, and even more desperate to marry an American, would often sleep with him for free.

"Do you think you're up to a hike, Helene?"

"At this point, Finster, I'm up for anything."

He looked at her curiously, then started gathering up the groceries, the bottled water, the hurricane lamp, and the Walkman. After stealing a glance outside to make sure that no one was around, he signaled Helene and his dogs to follow him. They trudged along a shaggy path through the jungle. At a white-knuckled boulder that looked as if it had punched its way out of the red dirt, they scrambled over a hill, then another and another, through scrub as thick as wool, as scratchy as mohair. At the bottom of the final incline, the scrub suddenly cracked open to reveal a viridescent cove with a slice of pink sand and a hut flanked by screw palms.

Finster hauled the supplies onto the hut's porch while Helene sat down on a bone-white piece of brain coral.

After shooing out the coconut crabs and airing out the hut, he told her he'd be back in twenty minutes with ice and a cooler, mosquito netting, fresh sheets, and whatever else he could think of.

"Thank you, Adam."

"Hey, no problemo."

He made two more supply runs, equipping the hut with enough canned goods to shame a bomb shelter.

When she finally asked him to stop, to forget about her, to get the Polaroids off to the Syrian, he trudged back to the village, but he didn't mail off the Polaroids to the Syrian. He didn't even phone the man. He promised himself he'd do it tomorrow. Instead, he returned to his room at Auntie Blukuk's guest house to prove to himself, and to Helene by proxy, that he wasn't at all what he appeared to be—a zonked-out kid at the ragged edge of the universe, but a man of unplumbed depths living out everyone's dream.

He took out the volumes of poetry he'd brought with him six years ago. The books were sheathed in Ziploc baggies, like paper food, for protection. He couldn't even remember when he'd read them last. D. H. Lawrence's *Sonnets and Verses,* Whitman's *Leaves of Grass, The Best American Poetry,* 1986 and 1987, W. H. Auden's *The Age of Anxiety,* and Elizabeth Bishop's *The Complete Poems.*

He picked up the Bishop, shook it free of its cellophane, and flipped it open:

Love's the boy stood on the burning deck
trying to recite "The boy stood on
the burning deck." Love's the son
stood stammering elocution
while the poor ship in flames went down.

Love's the obstinate boy, the ship,
even the swimming sailors, who
would like a schoolroom platform, too,
or an excuse to stay
on deck. And love's the burning boy.

He felt ill, ill from the beauty he'd never get near, ill from the knowledge that she'd be leaving, ill from the fact that he'd never let her leave, ill for being the boy on the burning deck and her the swimming sailor in the viridescent sea with only him for a rope and a lifesaver.

Save for dreams, when Thomas came to Helene unbidden, he hardly came back at all. Just before sleep, on the back of her closed lids, amid the pinwheels and hot spots of phosphors, she would try to reconstruct his face—a smudge of jaw, a blur of cheek, a back-lit face on the angled screen of a passing drive-in, as seen from the fast lane, before it dissolves into speed and headlights.

Supine, inert, immobilized, she'd hang on to that face, to that shadow graph thrown from the being of her Thomas, not quite able to believe that this was all she had left of him. Now, when there was no longer any reason to keep grief at bay, he wouldn't come back.

Try as she did, she could no longer call up his voice or his scent, and this, above all else, devastated her. Without a voice or a scent, Thomas had no presence, and without a presence, he was already calcifying into memory. This was untenable. She thought if she could just hear his voice, if she could just catch a whiff of him, she'd have the sense of his being near. But she had nothing of Thomas's left—not a pen or a watch or a button—that might still hold the ghost of him.

Only at dawn, after he'd made his cameo appearances in her dreams, trailing behind him the whole ardor of his being, did she experience a modicum of calm. With utmost caution, she'd stir herself from sleep and let her hand slide to the far side of the mattress, as though there was one chance in a million that she was not alone.

And she thought this was the worst of it.

But then a succession of firsts undid her.

The first deep sleep without Thomas, the first meal that was relished, the first walk where grief wasn't the point of the walk, the first momentary joy of the sun's warmth on her skin, the first absolute and undeniable hour in which his presence was completely absent, and not noticed, and finally, the first remembered dream in which Thomas didn't come back.

Had she been given a choice between this nothingness and grief, she would have chosen grief.

Mornings, Finster would arrive with fresh ice and his mooning gaze, but he was still better company than her own, or the seagulls, or the fistfuls of sand crabs, or the clockless nights during which she couldn't even evoke her dead husband's voice.

The boy talked a mile a minute.

His updates on their escape plans made no sense to her, but then again, little made any sense to her. Even the cove, with its shocking beauty, seemed so piteously ephemeral.

Finster was kind. Finster was gracious. Finster was the only human being she saw or spoke to. It was apparent how in love he was with her, or as in love as the man was capable of being. Shamed as she was to admit it, the little quirks of attention leavened the insufferable nights.

He blatantly craved her, and she didn't stop him. She told herself that a boy in love would do anything—and if she was to ever get out of here, she would need a boy who would do anything. But that was only a half-truth.

Ever since she'd been with Thomas, Helene had defined herself as a woman who was loved, and now she had no definition of herself. The fact that Thomas was dead, and he would never be conscious of her again—the petty, selfish, callow, incomprehensible fact that *he wasn't thinking about her* made the boy essential.

Finster was fiddling with something or other—the sweating

cooler, the sloshing ice. Night was dropping fast. A wind had already hopped up, thrashing the palm fronds to shreds. She didn't think she could bear to spend another night alone.

She sat down on the edge of the bed. "Stay," she said.

Finster looked at her with quizzical longing.

"I don't want to be alone tonight."

"Helene, I—"

"Don't say anything. Anything you say will be wrong."

Finster sat down beside her.

"Just hold me."

Finster held her.

"I want you to hold me till I fall asleep."

She stretched out, rolled onto her side, and faced the wall. Finster lay down beside her, spoon fashion, and tightly wound his arms around her. She let him hold her for a long time, but in the end, it wasn't enough. She turned over and took hold of his body, the stand-in body, the body by proxy.

He knew what she was doing. He could feel it in her touch. There was more attentiveness, more grace in that touch than he'd ever known or deserved. It was like someone caressing the ethereal blue heat that surrounds a body. It was the touch of a hand on a Ouija board. He made love to her with diligence and compassion. In order not to come too quickly, he thought of anything but her, he did mental inventories of his perfumes. Having never known love, he hoped that maybe love was transferable, that maybe the quotient of love in a being remained stable, and only the object of ardor changed.

They lay stock-still on the plank-wide cot. Finster didn't even allow himself to free his arm, despite his arm being crushed by her back, despite his arm becoming a block of burning ice. His head lay beside hers on the flat pillow. Her face was turned toward the wall. All he could see, in the shack's tenebrous shadows, was the whorl of her ear.

"Helene?"

She didn't answer.

"You okay?"

"Yes, no, I don't know."

"You probably don't want to hear this, but—"

"Please don't say anything, Adam."

"I love you."

"You don't love me. You only think you love me."

"It's a distinction I can't make, Helene." He pressed his brow against her damp neck; he could feel the spikes of her shorn hair. "I know my timing's shitty. I know you're probably still in shock over Thomas. But, say, in a while . . ." He could hear his own blood thudding in his ears. "Do you think you could love me?"

"I'm sorry, Adam, no."

"I'm not saying totally in love or anything. I'm saying you might begin to love me?"

"I'm sorry."

"I don't see how you can be so sure."

She turned over and cupped his face in her hands. This time it was very much *his* body she was touching—no ethereal blue heat here.

"My husband just died. I don't feel anything right now but unadulterated sadness."

For some mad reason, this gave him hope.

"There's no reason to make a rash decision, Helene."

She brushed the back of her hand across his cheek. He sank into her touch.

"I think you should go, Adam."

"You sure? You said you didn't want to be alone tonight."

"It's okay, really. I need to be alone now."

He lingered for a moment, his head suspended on her hand. He wanted to say something, anything that might elicit passion on her part, but he couldn't fathom what it could be. Finally, he sat up and reached for his shorts and flip-flops. Closing the door behind him, he walked to the end of the cove before reeling around and looking back. There was no moon, no illumination whatsoever, save for the phosphorescence marbling the waves. It looked like neon lightning being pressed upon the shore by a Titan's rolling pin.

The forged passport finally arrived, but Finster failed to mention it to Helene. He didn't think the Syrian had done a very good job. The photo was lopsided, the seal indecipherable, the print too small to read, even the cardboard blue cover seemed to have been made out of cheap construction paper.

The ferry was due the next morning. Helene hadn't slept with him again. She hadn't even allowed him to talk to her about it, or *them*, or *anything* that hinted at a future. Once on the boat, if they could even bribe their way onto the boat, he'd have only ninety-six pitching, sloshing, reeling hours before they arrived in Manila and she was gone.

He rummaged through his bare-bones soul and honestly concluded that he didn't think Helene was physically or emotionally up to the trip. Besides, he didn't think his plan was particularly sound. Whenever she asked him about the passport, he assured her it was coming. Whenever she asked him about the tickets or the schedule or the details, he assured her he was doing everything. On the morning of their supposed departure, when he trudged over the hill to supposedly fetch her, she was already waiting outside.

"Lucky I didn't have much to pack," she said, smiling.

"I'm sorry, Helene."

She shut her eyes, then opened them again. "Why are you sorry, Adam?"

"We can't leave today."

"What are you talking about?"

"Your passport hasn't come. The Syrian never showed up. I waited for him all morning." He felt light-headed, almost enervated by the lie, but he thought it would be easier on her this way.

She raked her eyes up and down him. "You said it would be here. You said the man was bringing it this morning."

"He never showed up. This is Vanduu, Helene, nothing works according to plan."

"I'm getting on the goddamned ferry, I don't care if I have a passport or not."

She started down the beach, walking along the murky edge of the surf. The tide had dropped three feet in the past hour and she immediately got bogged down, sinking up to her ankles in sand. For a minute or two, she hurled herself forward, hopelessly lifting one heavy, caked, sodden foot after another.

He grabbed her by her wrist. "You can't get on the ferry without a passport. It would be suicide, Helene."

She tried to wrench herself free, swearing vehemently at him, then abruptly quit and sank down in the brackish, sliding foam. The whole Pacific Ocean was draining away from her.

Finster squatted down beside her and gingerly put his arm around her. It seemed to him that when Helene was at her most fragile, he was at his very best. He helped her to her feet and walked her under the pinwheel shade of a palm. He sat her down and cradled her head against his shoulder.

"Listen to me," he said. "There'll be another ferry in three, four days. I swear to you, Helene, you'll have your passport by then."

"I can't take this much longer," she said, shaking her head as if to clear it of sea water. Then, slipping free of his grasp, she stood up and started pacing, but between the quicksand beach and the encroaching jungle, there was nowhere to go.

Finster swore to himself that he'd get her out of here.

But later that afternoon, alone in his room at Auntie Blukuk's, he knew he couldn't let her leave yet. Without her, without the hope of her loving him back, something vital within him would weld shut, and he'd become what he most feared, one of those bitter, craggy ex-pats, with a sullen hostitute on each tattooed arm, talking of glory days and the girls who got away. He watched as the last splays of dusk poked through the blinds. He'd only been alone for a couple of hours and already a breathy, jumpy panic had set in.

He rose from his cot, slipped on his trunks, and scrambled back over the path to Helene's, but he didn't dare knock on her door. She'd made it perfectly clear that she wanted to be alone tonight. Hanging back in the jungle scrub, he sat down on a rock and fished out a joint. Taking a toke for inspiration, he tried to conjure up a story, a teeny blur of truth that would make her believe that she couldn't yet leave. The ferry was stuck in Cebu? The ferry had broken down in Mindanao? The ferry had sunk in the Celebes Sea? Manila's harbor was being blockaded? A typhoon was twisting across the Pacific? He smoked and pondered until his brain went up in a conflagration of guilt. Crushing out his joint, he once again made the rickety resolve to help her escape.

Next morning, however, when he went to pick up her ice and breakfast, a most extraordinary spin of fate occurred. Mrs. Enin, the village scribe, was scrawling the village news on the chalkboard outside her video store. When Finster glanced over her shoulder, he saw her ancient hand rub out this week's ferry destination until *Manila* was no more than a smudge of chalk. Over it, in her palsied script, she wrote *Tim Tim*.

A renewed faith in the machinations of the universe restored him. He hurried back to Auntie Blukuk's just long enough to grab the forged passport (always feed a bitter pill with something sweet, his mother had told him), then trotted over the hill to tell Helene. But just before he stepped out of the jungle, he spied her standing at the lip of the ocean. Even from a hundred yards away, he could sense a part of her was already gone. He cautiously approached her and said he had both good news and bad.

"Give me the good news first, Finster, I need some good news."

"I have your passport."

"Thank God. And the bad?"

"The ferry's going to Tim Tim."

"I'll go to Tim Tim instead of Manila. What difference does it make?"

"You can't go to Tim Tim, Helene, it's East Timor. No one goes to East Timor, even with a real passport, let alone a forged one."

"When did you find this out, Finster?"

"Two seconds ago. They change the route and schedules all the time. It depends on what kind of cargo they've picked up, who wants what where. I swear to God, Helene, I just found out." Though he was telling the truth, for some inexplicable reason—a jolt of nerves perhaps—a tenuous smirk crossed his lips.

"Let me see my passport, Adam."

He handed her the passport. She stared at the flimsy blue cover, the shoddy binding, the lopsided picture, the seal that looked like a surprise decal found in a cereal box. "What is *this*? No one in their right mind is going to believe *this* is an American passport!"

"It's just a formality for the Vanduuan officials, Helene. I'm going to slip two hundred dollars into it."

His nervous smirk was now a frozen little shadow of itself.

"What are you pulling, Finster?"

"Helene, I'm not *pulling* anything."

"I don't believe you." She flipped through the passport again, then threw it at him. "What kind of game are you playing? What kind of fucking mind game are you playing?"

"Please, Helene," he said, scooping up the passport and dusting the sand off. "Try to calm down and listen to me."

"Calm down? Listen?" She was staring at him with such unbridled fury that it staggered him. "What possessed me to listen to you in the first place!"

The fragility that normally overtook her seemed nowhere around. He wasn't sure how to calm her. He tried to take her hand, but the violent recoil of her shoulders told him to stay away. "Helene," he said tentatively, "another ferry will be coming in a few—" He stopped, desperate to pick a date that she'd believe. "In two weeks."

"Get out!"

"Helene, please. You're not seeing the whole pic—"

"I said *get out now!*"

He turned toward the door, then reeled around, frantic to say something that would return her to a state of vulnerability, but all he could think of was, "I love you," and he knew that was exactly the wrong thing to say.

For the next few minutes, he loitered outside the shack, hoping that she'd come to her senses and try to find him. After all, if she thought about it, if she really, really thought about it, he was all she had. When he finally saw she wasn't budging, he jammed his fists into his pockets and scuffed along the high end of the beach, figuring that when he showed up tomorrow morning, with ice and breakfast, she'd have had time to see things more reasonably.

But on the way back to Pan'uu, on the top of the first hill, an abysmal despondency hit him. He couldn't quite fathom what had gone so wrong. After all, hadn't he been telling the truth this time?

Helene waited until midnight before gathering up her scant belongings—pocketbook, shroud, cigarettes, and Finster's Zippo. She blew out the hurricane lamp, but she didn't bother to shut the door. Giving wide berth to the hissing surf, she trudged along the edge of the jungle. At the foot of the hills, black and pointy as witches' hats, she braced herself, then started scrambling up the scratchy path into Pan'uu. Thorn bushes left strings of blood on her arms and legs.

The village was dark save for the embers of cooking fires and the occasional sweep of a moped's yellow headlamp, but Helene didn't need much light. She headed in the direction of the clanging generator.

Without bothering to disguise herself in any way, she hurried up the steps to tap on the office door of Motel Paradise. When no one responded, she tapped again, louder and more frantically.

In the recesses of the cinder-block building, a light flared and shuddered, then bobbed forward, penciling in all the chinks around the ill-fitting door.

It cracked open and Mr. Khan, unshaven, hair spiked and twisted as the blades of a blender, peered out, blinking rapidly in stunned unease. Behind him stood a pudgy Indian woman, also blinking rapidly, wearing a sarong like a cape.

"Mem Strauss?"

Helene nodded.

"Why have you come here? You have no right to come here."

Helene bowed her head, half in supplication, half in outright fatigue. "Please, may I come in?"

"I'm sorry, Mem Strauss. You must leave. Someone might see you."

Helene turned to the woman. "I need to ask your husband something important. I don't know anyone else to ask."

"My wife doesn't speak English."

Helene tried to take Mr. Khan's hand, but he stepped backward into the cement room. "I don't know where else to go, Mr. Khan."

The woman mumbled something to her husband and Mr. Khan shook his head skeptically. "You may come in for one moment, Mem Strauss. I cannot have you standing in full view of the village."

Helene followed the squat couple inside. The wife started shutting blinds, while Mr. Khan led Helene through the office into an interior room, a cement box within a cement box. There was a large, red, ornamental carpet on the floor, flanked by an ottoman and a Scotch-plaid sofa bed that looked as though it might have come from a Sears, Roebuck catalog circa 1957.

"My wife will bring you tea. What do you want from us, Mem Strauss?"

"I'm innocent. I wasn't even in the car. You knew my husband, Mr. Khan, you must know he didn't kill the child on purpose. It was an accident, a horrible accident. He was a good man, why would he kill a child?" She was speaking with utmost care and clarity, but every word ended in a ping of hysteria. By the time she finished, her voice was high-pitched and breathy.

"I am not the judge of your husband's actions, Mem Strauss."

"Why in God's name would Thomas kill a child on purpose!" she shouted, then abruptly fell silent, realizing how inappropriately loud her voice was.

"I don't believe he killed the child on purpose."

"Thank you," she said. And she reached out to lightly touch his arm.

Mr. Khan gently brushed her hand away. "You have not come here for my forgiveness. Why are you here, Mem Strauss?"

"I have money, Mr. Khan, lots of money in a bank at home. I can make you rich. You can have whatever you want, whatever you desire. You name the price, Mr. Khan. Any price. Just get me out of here, okay?" She was speaking in halting bursts, and she wasn't sure if she was making herself clear. "I know you know Vanduu. You travel across the borders to Kuantong and Minaphor all the time. You must know a way I can leave here. I have to leave here. I really, really, *really* have to get out of here. Look at me, Mr. Khan, I'm going crazy. You're the only one who can help me. I don't know anyone else to turn to. You're my last hope. If you won't help me, maybe I can buy a plan from you. Yes, yes, I'd be willing to buy a plan."

His wife appeared carrying a tea tray, and Helene stared at the brass pot, the delicate china cups and saucers, the pewter spoons with their intricate tooling, the little pyramid of brown sugar cubes, in stunned disbelief. It was as if the raw intimacy between her and Mr. Khan had been interrupted by a demure wife bearing civilization and all its accoutrements on a tea tray.

She knew the wife spoke no English—or, at least, they pretended she didn't—but Helene wasn't going to take any chances. She reached out and grasped the woman's wrist. "I'm going to make you and your husband rich, if only he will help me. You can have anything you want. I don't know what you want, but you can have it."

The wife set down the tea tray, then touched Helene's hand in a gesture of warning or kindness, Helene couldn't tell which. Finally she freed herself of Helene's grasp as deftly as one might shake off a bangle. She mumbled something to her husband, and Mr. Khan mumbled something back. Their language sounded like the gibberish one hears before fainting.

"You must excuse us for a moment, Mem Strauss. My wife requires my help in another room."

Mr. Khan accompanied his wife out, shutting the door behind them. Helene sank down on the Scotch-plaid sofa, then abruptly stood up and paced. When she couldn't face another cinder-block wall, she sat down again and tilted her head back. Exhaustion turned her limbs to sand. She thought if she had to run now, she couldn't do it. The couple was gone a long time—twenty, thirty minutes. Helene hadn't a clue. But it was long enough for them to have called the police, or the security forces, or the army, or whoever you call in Vanduu.

Finally the door opened and Mr. Khan came in alone. He sat down on the edge of the ottoman, and with great formality, gestured for Helene to have some tea.

Helene shook her head no.

"I will take you to Minaphor for five thousand American dollars, Mem Strauss."

Helene shut her eyes, then opened them again. "Oh my God, thank you, Mr. Khan. Thank you, thank you, thank you."

"May I offer you tea now? If you wish, my wife will bring a fresh pot."

Helene shook her head no. "Mr. Khan, you understand I can't pay you until I get home."

"I understand. You've made that quite clear, Mem Strauss. I will have to trust you, as you'll have to trust me." He poured himself a cup of tea, plopped in three sugar cubes, stirred vigorously, took a sip, shook his head, and added a fourth. "My wife pleads with me to cut down on my sugar."

"Aren't we leaving?"

"No one travels at night in Vanduu, except thieves and the army. We'll leave at dawn."

Now that the agreement seemed sealed, Helene felt pithed of

bone, drugged, hyper-calm. She'd be caught or she wouldn't be caught, he'd betray her or he wouldn't betray her—nothing she did or didn't do, said or didn't say, would make an iota of difference now. With the candor of the condemned, she asked, "Why are you doing this, Mr. Khan?"

"For the money, Mem Strauss."

"You could have asked for ten, twenty, a hundred thousand dollars."

Mr. Khan smiled. "Perhaps I made a mistake, but I believe I'm more likely to see the five." He swirled the tea in his cup, then tilted his head back and polished off the sugary dregs. "You should try to get some sleep, Mem Strauss. The sofa you're sitting on ingeniously opens up into a bed. Would you like me to open it for you?"

"It's not worth bothering, Mr. Khan. I doubt I'll sleep."

"I doubt that I'll sleep either, Mem Strauss."

He set down the cup, then braced his hands on his knees, as if to rise, but he didn't rise. Instead, he sank back on the ottoman and rubbed his eyes with both hands.

"My family is originally from Uganda, Mem Strauss. We lived there for three generations—first as railroad workers, then as shopkeepers. My father had an English haberdashery in Kampala. One day a madman, Idi Amin Dada, came to power. He killed tens of thousands, black and Indian, this one or that one, for no reason or for a reason that was so preposterous it wasn't a reason. If you wore English shoes, he killed you. If you looked a soldier in the eye, you were shot. If the soldier didn't want to waste a bullet, you were hacked to death with a machete. When the first wave of slaughter was over, he expelled all the Indians who were left, Muslim and Hindu alike. We were given hours to flee, we were allowed to take nothing. My wife had a sister in Fiji, so we moved to the other side of the world to begin again. The Fijians were a decent people at first, Methodists mostly, very religious, but then madness descended on Fiji, too. One day they were our neighbors, the next they were our enemies. My wife couldn't bear to become the object of hatred once again, and so we came to Vanduu. I have a bad feeling that madness is about to descend on Vanduu, and frankly, Mem Strauss, we simply cannot bear to begin again with nothing."

"Where will you go?"

He smiled, revealing his rust-red teeth. "Perhaps America. I understand you Americans have always been very kind to your immigrants."

"Things have changed, Mr. Khan. Don't count on it."

"I count on nothing, Mem Strauss."

Mr. Khan's plan was a marvel of simplicity. Helene would wear her shroud and head scarf and sit in the rear of the Paradise Tour van. The van's windows were tinted the color of moss. They would keep to back roads until a mile or so before the Kuantongan border. This way, if all went well, they'd avoid any in-country checkpoints, arbitrary roadblocks thrown up by soldiers in need of bribes. Just before the border, Mr. Khan would show Helene where and how to hide in a compartment behind one of the van's rear seats. He transversed this particular border crossing five or six times a month, and he knew all the guards. It was the route he used when he bussed wealthy Kuantongan ladies on illicit shopping sprees to Vanduu, where forbidden Western delicacies—whiskey and pirated American videotapes—were readily available. Normally, with a laugh and a small bribe—a bottle of whiskey, a carton of cigarettes—the guards would wave him through. Once in Kuantong, they'd head to the coast where most of the roads were paved. With any luck, it wouldn't rain, and they'd make it to the Kuantong River before nightfall. For ten American dollars, Helene could bribe a boatman to row her over to Minaphor. Once in Minaphor, she'd head straight to the American embassy and seek asylum.

On the seat beside Mr. Khan sat a case of Wild Turkey, eight slightly moldy cartons of Marlboros, and a bag of betel, into which, from time to time, he'd blindly grope while tenderly nursing the stubborn gear shift of the rust-drilled van. Helene sat three seats back, swathed in her shroud, keeping her head down, though the only person they'd seen in the past hour and a half—an elderly farmer under a heat haze of mosquitoes—barely looked up at them as they rattled by.

The roads were mostly dirt, or patches of tar in basins of mud, roads so off the beaten track, they *were* tracks, threadbare grooves in whirls of fern.

Neither spoke. Despite a polar dribble from the van's air conditioner, Mr. Khan's face was a sheen of sweat, his cheek, ballooned with betel, as shiny as a bowling ball. The border was another twenty-eight kilometers away.

The van began droning up the foothills, past taro flats hacked out of the jungle. Once they reached the full-blown mountains, they'd be forced to take paved roads, lest the van get mired on a muddy slope.

When Helene looked out now, all she could see were perpendicular wet green walls covered in slime and moss.

Mr. Khan crunched gears and the van shuddered up a steep incline, spewing mud and rocks in its wake. At the first paved road, a car-wide snake of asphalt, he cranked the wheel and they veered onto it.

Now and again, a wattle-and-thatch village suddenly popped out of the greenery, and Helene automatically crouched down, though the people in these border-disputed villages had long ago trained themselves not to look too closely at anything as officious as an opaque van careening through the back roads.

Once, coming round a blind bend, they came hood to hood with a jeep full of soldiers, but between the soldiers' Ray•Bans and the van's moss-colored windows, the two vehicles squeezed past each other without incident.

Finally, when it seemed the van couldn't climb any higher, Mr.

Khan pulled over onto a gravelly lookout with a tiny placard that said, SCENIC VIEW, in twelve languages.

Mopping his brow with a wadded hanky, he told Helene to stay put, set the emergency brake, slid out from behind the wheel, and trotted a hundred feet in one direction, doubled-back, and trudged a hundred feet in the other, all the while squinting down the heat-banded road.

When he was sure that no one was coming, he unlocked the van's side door, glided it open, rifled through his toolbox, and extracted a wrench and a pliers. He made another ineffectual swipe at his sodden face, this time using his shirtsleeve, then squeezed past Helene and crouched down in the gully behind her. He began unbolting the last row of seats. With a huff and a grunt, he hauled them forward to reveal a wedge of space the size of a child's coffin.

"I'm sorry, Mem Strauss, but this is the safest way." He made a beckoning gesture, as if he were inviting her onto a plush sofa, as opposed to a black hole.

Helene hitched up her shroud, climbed over the two rows of seats, then hunkered down and crammed herself in.

Mr. Khan fetched a black tarpaulin and covered her with it. The world shrank to blackness and her own breath. The tarp had been sitting next to the engine casing and smelled like a plastic plate left too close to a BBQ.

"Can you breathe all right?"

She shouted yes, as one might shout from the depth of a cavern.

"I shall try to be as quick as possible, but we have two border crossings to get through."

She could hear him huffing as he wedged the seat back into place.

"The guards see almost no one all day. They'll want to joke and chat. You must understand, Mem Strauss, I cannot rush them."

It was so horrifically stifling under the tarp that her mind couldn't adjust. She could actually feel her breath heat up the space with every exhalation. To keep herself from yanking off the tarp, she concentrated on a crack of light stranded next to her left foot. When the van lurched off, however, even that vanished, and she found herself hanging on to the van's every ping and whir.

She heard the engine sputter, the gears shift. She heard a fly, in its own state of panic, hurling itself against a window. The road sounded as though it was made of rock salt and flying glass, the brakes, when the van finally rolled to a stop, like a punctured balloon.

Mr. Khan cranked down his window and said something in Vanduuan. She didn't like the tone of his voice. It sounded insanely cheery, weirdly urgent. She knew he was handing out the bottles of Wild Turkey because one of the guards said, "Wild Turkey!"

Then she heard Mr. Khan lower his voice until it was scratchy and conspiratorial. He asked the guards if they'd heard the one about the Kuantongan official.

Evidently they hadn't because Mr. Khan prattled on.

"One day, a Kuantongan official visits his counterpart in Minaphor. The Minaphorian is living in great luxury—big house, big swimming pool, Filipina girlfriend. Amazed, the Kuantongan asks how he did it. The Minaphorian says, 'See that highway over there?' The Kuantongan sees a modern eight-lane highway. The Minaphorian says, 'Fifteen percent off the top.'

"The next year, the Minaphorian visits the Kuantongan official. He, too, is now living in great luxury—two grand houses, two big swimming pools, two Filipina girlfriends. The Minaphorian is shocked. He asks how he did it. The Kuantongan says, 'See that highway over there?' The Minaphorian sees only jungle. The Kuantongan says, 'One hundred percent!'"

The guards burst into raucous laughter.

Mr. Khan quietly said, "Good-bye, *vaya pergi tulu,*" goosed the accelerator, and the van sped away, only to come to a jerky stop a couple of seconds later.

Helene could actually hear him take a halting breath before jabbering something in a language that was a tad more guttural than Vanduuan. He no longer sounded charged and cheery, he sounded drained.

The clink of glass filled the van as more bottles of Wild Turkey were passed out.

Then, in a voice as conspiratorial as before, but with a little less urgency, a little more sighing, Mr. Khan asked the guards if they'd heard the one about the Vanduuan official.

Evidently they hadn't because Mr. Khan droned on.

"One day, a Vanduuan official visits his counterpart in Minaphor. The Minaphorian is living in great opulence—vast estate, big swimming pool, many wives. Amazed, the Vanduuan asks how he did it. The Minaphorian says, 'See that highway over there?' The Vanduuan sees a modern eight-lane highway. The Minaphorian says, 'Fifteen percent off the top.'

"The next year, the Minaphorian visits the Vanduuan official. He, too, is now living like a sultan—two grand estates, two big swimming pools, one hundred wives. The Minaphorian is shocked. He asks how he did it. The Vanduuan says, 'See that highway over there?' The Minaphorian sees only jungle. The Vanduuan says, 'One hundred percent!'"

For a moment, Helene thought she'd gone mad, that the van had never moved from the first spot, that Mr. Khan was telling the same joke again, that, like a bad comedian, he'd tell it for eternity, ad nauseum, until her skin became welded to the hot, airless tarp. But then the van suddenly lurched off again, this time at a rapid clip, and didn't stop until it sounded as if they'd glided into the jungle. Palm fronds, like the brushes of a car wash, scraped the van's roof and fenders.

Helene didn't dare move or say anything until the seat was wrenched forward and the tarp pulled off. She sat up, gasping.

"We're now in Kuantong, Mem Strauss. Would you like some ice water?"

"Thank you, Mr. Khan," she said, hauling herself up and reeling. She could see he wanted to help her, but he didn't dare touch her. She climbed over the seat, then sank down on the van's orange shag carpet a foot or two away from him. "I'd love some ice water."

"If you'd be kind enough to hold the cups," Mr. Khan said, handing her two plastic cups. He uncapped a small thermos, carefully poured out the water, and they gulped it down with abandon, side by side, in the underwater light of the moss-tinted windows.

Fifteen minutes later, they were wending their way down a mountain as sheer, slippery, and dripping as the hull of a capsized ship, toward a valley as rolling as breakers. As far as Helene could see, everything—the lichen-covered rocks, the moss-shrouded telephone poles, the vine-clotted trees—was a variation of green: clover, algae, pea, thalo, veridian, and lime. She was once again seated behind Mr. Khan, one sandaled foot folded under her. He was steering with both hands, chomping on betel, trying, as discreetly as possible, to expel its vermilion juice into a small pewter spittoon that was shimmying on the dash.

"Do you mind if I smoke?" she asked.

"For myself, no. But if someone should see you . . . Kuantongans are very religious. It isn't appropriate to smoke in public while wearing hijab."

"Perhaps I should try betel."

"Perhaps." She thought she caught the barest hint of a vermilion smile in the rearview mirror. "But it often makes people extremely nauseous on their first attempt."

They drove on in silence.

By the way he kept craning his neck to check the fish-eyed landscape scrambling past in the side-view mirror, she knew he was still nervous. From time to time, he'd blurt out one inconsequential tour guide fact after another, just as a pianist, in moments of dire stress, might play, on the air itself, an ethereal riff. She could sense he was desperate to talk. Whenever they passed the barest shell of a landmark—an ancient wall, a rusted cannon—he insisted on recounting its sad history.

She didn't want to hear it. Any of it. She had no curiosity left. Tilting her temple against the window glass, she only half listened, just enough to catch tidbits about conquerors in creaking armor and Portuguese ships laden with rats and pestilence, or mythological Kuantongan half-beasts, as strong as Mr. Atlas, as agile as Spider-man, slaying enemies with potions and prayer.

They rolled into a Kuantongan town. It looked exactly like a Vanduuan one, but without any advertisements. A policeman in a dirty white uniform and dirty white gloves was directing traffic.

"Please keep your head down, Mem Strauss, we're not out of danger."

She slouched down until all she could see of the town were the tops of spartan gray apartment houses strung with flapping laundry. The occasional goat brayed on a balcony.

They rolled back into the jungle, past a smoking field, then veered left and skirted black mangrove swamps and stilt fishing villages and hardened lava runoffs that looked like melted record vinyl.

According to Mr. Khan, each village was a vale—no, a whole gulf—of tears. She tried to blot out his voice by concentrating on the whine of the air conditioner, but a few snippets filtered through. When the Portuguese were done, the Spanish missionaries sailed in, offering Baptism or beheading. Then the top of a volcano blew, incinerating Muslim and Catholic alike. When the smoke died down, the Dutch swung by for rubber, the Germans for copra, the English for phosphate, the Americans for military bases and glory.

By the time the Japanese showed up for WWII, there were hardly any natives left to enslave.

The van coughed, then climbed to the crest of a hill. In the distance, past acres of stumps and a chrome-tinted river, lay a huge modern city, all geometry, glass, and strip malls, in its own little bubble of smog. Between the retro-seventies skyscrapers and its ruler-straight boulevards, Helene thought she was hallucinating.

"Minaphor, Mem Strauss."

Mr. Khan jimmied the shift, easing the van into low gear, and they glided down toward what looked like Orlando, Florida, or downtown Anaheim. For a moment, Helene couldn't quite bear to look at it, knowing how much Thomas would have loved the architectural incongruities, the global hodgepodge.

Once on flat land again, the city vanished behind the stump-cut hills and a fence of jungle. All she could see of it was the tinsel-tinted blush of smog.

They began paralleling the river, where Kuantongan women, shrouded in hijab, squatted on boulders, washing thirty-foot bolts of batik patterned with psychedelic sunbursts and trumpet-shaped plants. Around one convoluted bend, where the river widened majestically, they came to a break in the trees. Minaphor was now clearly visible, but from this short distance, a half mile of water, it didn't seem so citified. The buildings looked dinkier, the architecture more like a Southern California shopping mall than a full-fledged urban sprawl. There were tar-paper shacks on both banks. Dugout canoes, tipped and laden with Kuantongan passengers, were poled back and forth by Minaphorans.

Mr. Khan pulled off the road, killed the engine, and told Helene to wait in the van. Sliding out, he stood for a moment in a hazy flare of late-afternoon sun, wiping his face with his hanky, before approaching one of the boatmen. The man sat hunkered in his canoe, sporting a T-shirt that said *No Radio in Car*. Mr. Khan squatted beside him, and for a moment it appeared as if they were arguing vehemently. Then both men shook hands and Mr. Khan, tenuously bracing himself on the wobbly edge of the boat, rose to his feet and walked back to the van.

He slid open the side door and climbed in beside her.

"The man will take you to Minaphor for eight American dollars. Your embassy is only a short walk from the river."

"I don't have eight dollars," Helene said.

Mr. Khan gave her a handful of Vanduuan coins. "This should buy your passage, Mem Strauss." He smiled. "You needn't add that to my payment." He reached into his pocket and dug out a slip of paper with a slew of numbers and a Barclays Bank address. "I keep an account in Minaphor. If you could wire the money directly there. Please, whatever you do, Mem Strauss, don't send it to Vanduu."

"I won't send it to Vanduu," Helene said. She slipped the piece of paper into her pocketbook. She knew not to touch him, but she placed her hand a millimeter away from his on the Naugahyde backrest. "Thank you, Mr. Khan. Thank you for everything."

"Sama-sama."

She climbed out of the van and started walking.

"Mem Strauss," Mr. Khan called after her, "I'm very sorry about your husband."

"So am I."

She stepped into the canoe, sat down in its hacked-out stern, and poured the coins into the boatman's hands. After counting them with irksome exactitude, the man jabbed his pole into the translucent water, setting off a mini-whirpool of muck, and they slowly inched across to the other side. He dropped her off in a foot of water and she waded ashore.

Once in Minaphor, she started walking, almost running. The streets edging the river, if you could call them streets, had the same strapped squalor as Vanduu, but once she reached the first major boulevard, the city abruptly transformed. The sidewalks became as wide and white as suburbia's, the building facades, save for streaks of jungle rot around the gutters, as immaculate as a theme park's. Palms studded the curbs, each exactly the same height, each coiffured into a perfect bouffant. For a moment, Helene felt as if she'd crashed through the friable membrane of shock into dream.

She slowed down and joined the ranks of pedestrians, Chinese women in nylons and pumps, Chinese men in business suits with diamonds of sweat on their backs. At one intersection, already heating up in her shroud, she stopped a young girl to ask where the American embassy was.

Looking completely flummoxed by the white face and American accent coming out of the Muslim head scarf, the girl said that she wasn't exactly sure, but that most of the embassies were on General MacArthur Boulevard. She spoke flawless English but with incomprehensible inflections. From what Helene could make out, in order to get to the embassy, she could either walk several blocks around a turnabout or cut through Queen Victoria Mall, the big stucco shopping complex on her left.

Helene cut through Queen Victoria Mall. It wasn't at all queenly or Victorian, it had a futuristic theme—pink and orange neon lights, a Plexiglas fountain, escalators with purple handrails. Peeling off her head scarf, Helene experienced real air-conditioning for the first time in weeks—not a blast of Sub-Zero Freon, or a trickle of tepid breath, but true immersion into relief. She sat down on a bench. The bench wore a large sign with a roster of warnings: NO GUM CHEWING, NO DURIANS, NO SPITTING, NO SMOKING, NO LOITERING, NO LEPAK. PERMISSION TO SIT IS FOR TEN MINUTES ONLY! Helene ignored the sign. She shut her eyes, then opened them again, stunned to find herself facing a lineup of universal mall shops—the CD store beside the Levi's blue jeans outlet set against the Kentucky Fried Chicken standing next to the electronic-gizmo warehouse—an equation for commerce as global as geometry. It was spectacularly comforting, and for the first time since she could remember, she actually felt safe. She knew she should get up and make her way to the embassy, but she couldn't quite get herself to move. Closing her eyes once again, she tilted her head back against the bench and allowed herself a few crucial moments to luxuriate in the temperate climate of the mall and its weirdly American smells—a waft of frying chicken and something lovelorn like cheap Woolworth perfume.

Part Three

Finster surveyed the long volcanic stretch of beach and spotted a tiny figure hurrying toward him. In the low-slung sun, the figure looked incidental compared with its colossal shadow. Against the black sand and the shimmering sea, all Finster could make out was a speck of mortal matter in a flapping white shirt and tie.

Finster ignored the man and looked up at the red-violet sky. He was wholly, miserably, nerve-rackingly sober. Ever since Helene had disappeared four nights ago, smoking pot had only induced a blitz of paranoid memories and bathetic fantasies. Sober, he was able to accept the plain, hard fact that he'd lost her, and she wasn't coming back.

Matter of fact, he was standing on the beach just then because, according to Parker, his one reliable source, she was flying home that evening on a big jumbo jet and Pan'uu was on the flight path. The Minaphorans had finally agreed to release her: They wanted her out of their country before her case became an international cause célèbre. Within the past twenty-four hours, her story had been picked up by the *Herald Tribune,* the *Jakarta Post,* the *Straits Times.* The Americans could hardly send her back to Vanduu now. Speculations about her escape abounded in the Vanduuan press, but most of the guesses were so ludicrous—a U.S. submarine, a CIA operation—that no one paid them any heed. Only after Finster had spotted the tiny FOR SALE sign on Motel Paradise, did he put the pieces together.

He sat on the beach, absently picked up a sliver of driftwood, and drew the outline of a woman in the sand. He lay down beside her. Stars were just beginning to appear across the violet and pink diorama. In the lighter streaks of mauve, funnels of sunlight, all chromatics and glitz, shot out from behind silver-tooled clouds. Finster took in every square inch of beauty searching for the jet, but whatever majesty was up there no longer awed him.

Without love, or the promise of love, Finster had lost his foggy yearnings.

His dogs had sensed the change in him and tried, dog-fashion, to bring him back. They followed him incessantly, compulsively licked his hands, and tried to demonstrate, by their sheer exuberance in minuscule pleasures—a rotting coconut, a putrid fish head—that life was worth living.

The figure hurrying toward him was now close enough for Finster to make out who it was, the American missionary boy, Mr. Millennium. The boy had recently fallen in love with a fourteen-year-old Vanduuan girl, a convert, and he desperately needed a bottle of Finster's perfume to make her take note of him. Had the old Finster been around, he'd have teased the boy mercilessly about giving credence to such a heretic potion, but not now. Finster finally understood what he'd been selling all along. He stood up, leaving his footprints on the spot where the outlined woman's heart would have been, if she'd had a heart, and led the boy to his Quonset hut.

Clad in pink sarongs with matching pink Yves Saint Laurent jackets, the stewardesses on Minaphor Airlines hand out steaming face towels and polyester slippers before the jet even takes off. As soon as it's airborne and they can safely pop out of their seat belts, they serve hot hors d'oeuvres and bright tropical drinks, each with a matching bamboo umbrella stabbed into its icy froth.

Helene accepted everything—the hot towel, the Mai Tai, the shrimp on a skewer—all the while looking down through the pitted Plexiglas window at Vanduu. In the waning light, she could just make out the checkerboard rice paddies, the charred swatches of slash-and-burn farms, the smog shrouding the capital, under which so much chaos and misery teemed. Yet something about the plastic-scented air in the plane's cabin, the servility of the smiling stewardesses, even the festive bamboo umbrellas, seemed so sterile by comparison.

She sank back in her seat and thought about home. It was one sorrow she hadn't allowed herself to venture anywhere near. In truth, she couldn't imagine how she'd get through the first few minutes in the empty apartment, let alone the next few months. She couldn't fathom opening the front door to the untouched, unchanged rooms that she and Thomas had left in disarray—his shirt on the bed, his imprint on the sheets, his robe on the floor.

Just before they'd locked the front door, Thomas had asked her if he should rinse out their half-finished coffee cups, and she'd flippantly said no, they'd see what grew in them while they were gone, what new little world they'd give birth to. Of all the sorrows facing Helene, it was the thought of seeing these two coffee cups, with their embryonic vestiges of life, that devastated her.

She pressed her cheek against the cold Plexiglas and watched Vanduu slide beneath the silver wing of the jumbo jet and disappear.